PRAISE FOR PATRICIDE

"In D. Foy's *Patricide*, the prose is so sharp and evocative that I feel as if I'm watching camcordered home movies that I both treasure and fear. It is as if Denis Johnson wrote *Jesus' Son* with an anvil. There is blood and violence and there is heartbreak and heat and there is life and death on these pages. This book is a conjuring even as it is a killing."

—*Linsday Hunter*

"Those of us who've been following D. Foy's writing for a while will be gratified to find, in *Patricide*, another marvel of emotional intelligence, another heady cocktail of high linguistic invention and vernacular speech. Foy's writing contains such energy, such sheer firepower, it's tempting to cast him as a word merchant in the Stanley Elkin vein, a superlative technician working in the dark American shadow of Melville, etc. Only—such a description would omit Foy's greatest virtue, namely, his wisdom. It's one thing to describe the bleaker corners of experience with such full-throated vitality, and yet quite another to do so with as much empathy and equipoise. I already knew Foy was a genius. Now I'm beginning to think he's a saint."

—*Matthew Specktor*

"*Patricide* is a torrent: bruising, beautiful, impossible to shake. D. Foy writes with an intelligence and a ferocity that is exquisitely his own."

—*Laura van den Berg*

"Biting as Beckett and honey-hued as a Tom Waits ramshackle ballad, *Patricide* is a spiraling and spiteful spire of memory's two great gods, nostalgia and blame. With it, Foy has delivered a true work of art—addictive, hypnotic, relentless."

—*Scott Cheshire*

"*Patricide* is a novel of abuse, addiction, and conflicted love in which D. Foy bends language around the patriarchal until it screams. It's a knockout of a book. Read it now."

—*Terese Svoboda*

"The fraught relationship between fathers and sons has been poured over by the likes of Rick Moody, Ivan Turgenev, Steven King, Pat Conroy, Philip Roth, and Cormac McCarthy. What D. Foy does in *Patricide* is blast fully into the ranks of the masters. A frightening, touching, challenging, and emotionally charged masterpiece."

—*Christian Kiefer*

"I'm a fan of Foy, not just for the crazy tales he cooks up, but for his formidable use of language. He writes sentences that are both beautiful and volatile at the same time. *Patricide*, like a lovely concussion, will leave you dizzy and desperate for the next page."

—*Joshua Mohr*

"The literary superstorm that is *Patricide* reads as though it had been brewing for decades before D. Foy, in a torrent of inspiration, was forced to blow. As Karl Ove Knausgaard explodes life's quotidian moments with cool, clockworkprecision, Foy expands phenomena ecstatic and traumatic to degrees that not only evoke lived experience but transport the reader to their very essence. When finally the novel achieves its full cyclonic shape, you're caught in its horrid eye, confronted with the kind of diamond-cut awareness typically offered only to the broken, the abused, the fully-surrendered. The screaming inner child—help me, save me, love me—is torn to bits, giving rise to a quietude that demands nothing less than acceptance of things as they are. Foy's been there, and lives there still, and this book offers up his battered jewel."

—*Sean Madigan Hoen*

"Warning: This book, *Patricide,* is not messing around. This book is going to take you with it. Do not fight this book, it will win. This book will bite, but you will like it. This book will hurt, but in the best of ways. Do not be afraid of this book. Be thankful D. Foy has made it for us."

—*Elizabeth Crane*

"Hurricane Father rips through the pages of *Patricide.* We stand there stunned, surveying the wreckage, only to realize that this is just the eye: another wall of storm is coming— Hurricane Mother, Hurricane Addiction, Hurricane Marriage. D. Foy animates and maps these weather systems of life, but he's less a meteorologist in a studio than a storm chaser with his head out the window of a van, screaming brilliance dead into the wind."

—*Will Chancellor*

9/12/17

ABSOL UTELY GOLDEN

A Novel

D. FOY

**ST.L
KNG
HRS
PRS**

STALKING HORSE PRESS
SANTA FE, NEW MEXICO

ABSOLUTELY GOLDEN

First paperback edition published by Stalking Horse Press, September 2017

The characters and events in this book are fictitious. Any similarity to real persons, living or dead, is coincidental and not intended by the author.

www.stalkinghorsepress.com

Design by James Reich
Author Photograph by Snorri Sturluson

Stalking Horse Press
Santa Fe, New Mexico

Stalking Horse Press requests that authors designate a nonprofit, charitable, or humanitarian organization to receive a portion of revenue from the sales of each title. D. Foy has chosen Mid-Atlantic Bully Buddies.

www.midatlanticbullybuddies.org

For Jeanine

ABSOLUTELY GOLDEN

Illegitimati non carborundum.

In the summer of 1953, when I was eighteen, I gave myself to a boy beneath an old pecan, in a field by the refinery. We lay in the grass, sweating, a compote of scents in my head, us and earth and oil. A whir filled the air. Birds were reeling high above.

"I didn't know eagles lived around here," I said.

The boy picked a twig from my hair. "They don't," he said. "Those are vultures."

The sun was shining, the birds were singing, the bees were buzzing—*buzz, buzz, buzz*—and I was completely naked.

Children ran to touch me. Men and women stared. I glowed with smiles, like joy embodied, like nothing, I'm sure, they'd seen. For the very first time I introduced myself. I held their hands, I bore their jokes, I told them who I was.

Hadn't we met before? they said. *Perhaps at Davenport Landing or Santa Cruz. Had I witnessed* XB-58?

That was it, they said, *yes,* they said, *they'd seen me in the pages of* LIFE.

And when I told them that this was my unveiling, so to speak, that I'd never been even to a public pool, they were dazed.

But it can't be! they said.

Hey, Rachel, they said, *aren't you thirty-eight?*

And you wear your self so well, they said. *Have you ever worn a bra?*

Super, they said.

Cool, they said. *Incredibly outrageously fantastic!*

Isn't it? I said, and twirled.

17

I'd been wrong about Camp Freedom Lake, obviously.

But for its "policies"—on the surface, at least—it was a spot like any other, circled by redwoods and mountains, plush with cottages, a clubhouse, and the "Chuck Wagon," as they called it, for meals and snacks.

And volleyball courts and shuffleboard courts, these, too, were there, plus a playground and pool that, according to the American Sunbathing Association's inaugural poll of '73, was the largest for nudists in the country, probably in the world. There were picnic tables, horseshoe pits, great spans of lawn, everything, really, from solariums to wading pools, Parchesi boards to pergolas, an honest-to-goodness Shangri-la.

Three hundred forty-two people—salesmen, housewives, nurses, and cooks, janitors and mechanics, models and guards, a soccer pro from France—had gathered to this place, what I wouldn't see till later was in fact a realm of fairy-dust enchantment. Cut out of California, like a dream adrift, Camp Freedom Lake, truly, was Shangri-la, and someway, how true, I had stumbled on its magic—Shangri-la, Shangri-la.

But though I was naked now, not an hour before I'd stood at the mirror anxious and confused.

By what force had I been brought here, by what wound in the fathomless dark?

I'd broken my wrist as a child and gone with a cast for months. Worse than the wound was the itch that seemed never to end, plus the stink when they took the cast. A girl had run out to greet me as we pulled up at home, but seeing my arm, she plugged her nose. *It looks like a cucumber*, she said.

I wore sweaters that summer, and for years after that, and became obsessed with lepers, and waited for the Russians' bomb.

We suffer, we people, we do. We carry secrets we know nothing of, and harbor them even, and sometimes even nurture for life. And we keep this torment because we deserve it, or believe we do, because, really, nearly always, we feel guilty.

Yet what is this guilt but our belief that somehow, somewhere, we've been badly judged?

And what is that belief but our misled acceptance of this judgment?

My father, God rest his soul, was a lovely man: he was never there to make more children with my mother. As for her, if neglect were a virtue, she'd have been the wife of a king. *Eagle Beak*, she called me, her one and only girl. *Macula Mouth, Jaw Breaker, Weed Head*, and on.

For Christmas one year I found in my stocking a bottle of witch hazel, together with a packet of swabs.

If someone came to the door when my father was away, my mother scurried to her room.

Make a peep, she'd hiss, *and you're dead meat!*

And so it's true: we spend our lives in need of praise, yet when at last we're handed the key to freedom, what do we typically do but toss it in a ditch?

My husband was dead these long years—twelve, poor Clarence!—and I'd been hurled, invisible, to the bottom of the pit of the cursed to search for explanations, endlessly, it seemed, pathetically, I know, till at last that ancient gypsy sold me her potion for love.

"Is no funny," she'd said when I gagged at her orders, and even, a little, laughed. Earthworms and periwinkle, Spanish flies, menstrual blood, leeks? "This is very old, very strong. Man will come, I promise."

Ah! If only she'd lied, the witch—because she hadn't, not a worthless speck.

Three days later, just as she'd said, he slipped through my Oakland door, this hippie named Jack, and started in on Freedom Lake. The parasite! The potion and its spell—what else could it have been?—had bound me to this gangly dolt as surely as my curse had kept the vilest men at bay.

So when Jack said appearances were the last thing at a nudist camp anyone should fret, I was too deluded to see the import of that notion, too fanatically obsessed with what I'd taken for years for needs. I was, I now know, living an exercise in futility whose principle thrust lay in maintaining some coherence before a contradiction I could never square. And though the contradiction itself lay in my "relationship" with Jack, and though I was nothing if not a willing mark, I have to say he did have a way with things, even, I might add, if he didn't quite know just what it was he said.

Jack, essentially, wanted something other than I'd been. But I couldn't give him that, then. I'd rather slink down the street with a rash on my face, I told him, than leave the house without my do. Besides, the thought of packs of loafers idling round in lewd undress—there was that, as well. Honestly, I said, the whole thing filled me with the kind of fear I'd only known near public baths and chemistry labs.

One of Jack's ploys revolved around convincing me that my *worries, man*, were merely the by-products of our *like corporatized America*.

Another was *like nature*. If we were going to lounge naked for weeks in the Humboldt woods, who would care what kind of coiffure my stylist might swing?

Plus sure he was lying, but Jack must've told me fifty times over he'd like me better without my *Uncle Sam hair*.

"*Au naturel*, Rachel-baby," he'd say. "Like that's where it's at."

And anyway, he said, *the dudes where we were headed weren't going to waste their time worrying they'd like seen me on the cover of* Cosmopolitan. *The chicks, either,* he said.

One day Jack even had it in him to say they wouldn't care if my head was bald as a baby rabbit.

"These cats we're going to hang with," he said, skinny like a wretch, "are righteous."

I knew he was using me—down at Earl's Odyssey of Hair, Judy, Lena, Georgina, and Juaquina never let up on that—but still I couldn't flee him, to speak of the attempt. I couldn't, in truth, somehow, do any but what he said.

"I hate to say it," Judy had told me over and again, "but if it weren't for how you care for him, that guy would've scrammed the week after you took him in."

"I mean for real," Georgina said. "What's a crazy buck like him want with some old widow?"

"Rachel," said Juaquina, "she is a good woman. And Jack, he is a good man. Sometimes he is."

"Ha!" Georgina said. "You don't think he's got some other piece of tail while she's slaving in her class with those nasty little whelps?"

"Rachel is no bag of bones," Juaquina said. "None of us is that."

"Yeah, well," Lena said, "for whatever my two cents is worth, we're no bag of cherries anymore, either."

It took a year and a half, but at last I submitted, I agreed to Jack's thing with the nudists, believing, for a while anyway, that I could do it. Which wasn't to say I'd changed my mind about changing my hair. Already I'd given Jack more than he deserved. He would have to take what he could get.

Then the last day of school came round, a week before we left for camp, and Abel Rich, the worst of my many rotten students, bullied Rhonda Lynn, and I ripped out a clump of his pretty blond hair, and my world was indisputably altered.

One minute he was crouched above the fountain, the brat, the next his head snapped back, the hair in my fingers, creepy with flecks of blood. And not even after I'd made it to Earl's, and Judy had given me a nip of gin, did that polluted vision let me be.

I knew only that I'd changed.

"Let's do something different today," I said to Judy, while the ladies all stared.

"Different?" she said. "Like what kind of different?"

"I saw a picture of Bubbles Wilson."

"Bubbles who?" Lena said.

"The most beautiful blonde on Broadway. She was a Zeigfeld Follies girl. In the '20s. Make it ready for *au naturel*. You know. Big and long and curly."

"I can do that just fine," Judy said, holding my hair like it was fur. "What do you want to do with this mousy brown?"

It had been a few years since I'd last had a cut, though no one would know by the way Judy fixed it each week, between a bouffant and tossed-up bun. I had the length, all right.

"Dye it, of course."

"Blonde?"

"I know you'll all find this hard to believe, but I'm going to be a child of the sun."

Judy might as well have turned my hair to fire.

She spun me round, and every word fell short. Above the whirring of dryers a singer sang, *Schoooool's—out— for—sum-mer!*

Lena stuttered. "It's . . . it's . . ."

"It's *muuuy* bonita, Rachel!" Juaquina said.

"Damn, girl," Georgina said, and stared. "*Damn*."

Bubbles Wilson had nothing on me.

My hair was a great golden downpour of trumpets and flames, gold as the goldest dates.

I imagined myself in the sun. Jack would shudder when I spoke, or maybe weep and sing. And if the proper sigh should escape my lips, Jack would do murder, be murdered, too. In a dream, he could eat my hair, should

I deign to let him, and my hair would taste like secrets. At night, from another room, he'd moan.

In truth, I rushed off from Earl's eager for Jack's support, but got instead music blasting from my house, and the tittering of a boozy girl. I expected it to be the trollop this hippie friend of Jack's always brought along, Halo or Fay or Layla, whatever the heck it was. I expected to hear the hippie himself.

A breeze had risen, the smell of mesquite and steaks. Across the way, a boy was fouling his stoop with chalk.

When she gets there she knows, went the song, *if the stores are all closed, with a word she can get what she came for. Oooh-oooooh!*

And then, at last inside, what should I find but the girl I'd heard, lying on Jack with her skirt up her legs, practically to the waist.

"Jacky," she shouted, and jolted to her feet, "you didn't tell me your mother was stopping by?"

She was so dark with sun she could've been a girl you see in the movies with Frankie and Annette. Her hair was long and smoothly straight, and moreover it was blonde. She feigned at stepping forward and extended a golden hand.

"It's nice to finally meet you, Mrs. Gammler?"

I started for the kitchen, into which Jack had conveniently crept. "Jack?"

"Rachel-baby," he said, reappearing with a gin and tonic and his smugly bearded face.

But for the can of soup he'd warmed when I had the flu, Jack had never once offered me a thing, much less *served* me.

"I thought you'd dig a slurp off the old juniper juice," he said, "you know, after a hard day of slaving for the master and all. Courtesy of Chez Gammler. So Jenny," he said, turning to the girl, "check out Rachel. Rachel, this here is like my cousin Jenny."

I knew it best to let my eyes do my work. I stared Jack down and waited.

"You know," Jack said, "I told you about her last week?"

"You mean this is your *roommate*?" said the girl with a jiggle of her breasts, scarcely contained, I realized, by the top of her bikini.

"Dig it." Jack held out his arms like a game show host. "The one and only Rachel-baby, *in the flesh*."

"I'm sooooo sorry? I don't know why, but when Jacky told me about you I had a *completely different picture*?"

"Whoaaa," Jack said, his face gone flat. "Your *hair*, man. Like what did you do to your *hair*?" He turned back to the girl. "Will you dig her *hair*?"

"It's pretty far out," said the girl.

"But seriously," Jack said, "check it out. It's kind of *real* looking."

The next thing I knew the little moll had taken up my hair. "But just wait till you touch it!" she said.

"What did you say your name was?" I said.

"Jennifer? But Wacky-Jacky here just calls me Jenny?"

Jack crammed the last of his doobie in an alligator clip, then stood there sucking at the thing.

"I forgot to tell you," he squeaked. "Jenny's coming with us to camp."

The Ecdysiast—this, absurdly, being the name for

what Jenny repeatedly said was her "profession"—ran her hands along her hips and breasts.

"Last summer on Fermentera," she said, "was the most liberating experience I've ever had? We didn't even have to complain about what a drag the *Tex*tiles were, you know, because there was a ban on them. It was fan*tas*tic. I mean, the sense of, I don't know, *free*dom I guess, was fan*tas*tic?"

"Rock and roll," Jack said.

"I don't recall any of this," I said.

"I'm sure you've gone there plenty?" The Ecdysiast said.

"Excuse me?"

"That's one of the advantages of age—*freedom*?"

"I'm a teacher," I said. "I teach children."

"The nude beaches on the Med are *so* boss," The Ecdysiast said.

"Did you forget to tell me something?" I said to Jack.

He put his hand on my arm and coughed. "Mellow out, man, and drink that juice I made you."

"Just think, Rachel," The Ecdysiast said, "the only thing you've got to pack is your *toothbrush*!"

"It's cool, Jenny," Jack said. "Rachel, you know, she gets a little uptight if she doesn't know when the program begins and ends."

"I used to be that way, too?" The Ecdysiast said.

"You were so uptight," Jack said. "Like a *suit*, man, yeah."

"But you took out *all* the kinks, didn't you, Jacky?"

Jack held up his hands and wriggled his fingers. "Some of us got it and some of us don't."

This man had not bewitched me. That much by then I knew. I'd simply fallen into him, as a child to a well, like my gypsy had said. I'd done his bidding from the instant he appeared, and was doing it still.

And now here I was at his nudist camp, after all, taking off my clothes as though to another spell yet, exposing my average-woman's legs and average-woman's hips, my belly and buttocks and spine, straight as truth, I had to admit, after years without love, without my dear lost Clarence and all the things my Clarence had loved, in the pall of stations, the shade of parks, our room.

Just what was it that terrified me so?

I was only thirty-eight—young, or youngish, maybe, one heck of lot better off than most folks my age. My buttocks hadn't fallen the way some women's had, and my breasts were firm. Plus I had my hair, now, beautiful and blonde and luxuriously long.

And hadn't I told the girls I was a child of the sun? *The rays of the sun,* I once read, *are like the hair of the gods.*

But the people here at camp weren't gods, though for all their flaws they dallied and pranced like Pan with his lute. Which was the point, of course, I knew—to give the lie to society's rule to forever wear our shame. Because what was a bathing suit, as one of Jack's magazines opined, if not *the world's most useless article of clothing, a functionless, illogical, soggily clinging trap, designed, apparently, for the express purpose of keeping cold wet fabric plastered to human skin?*

Once I was a woman at a grave.

Now I was a circus, and a girl, real.

The lights were spangling, the crowd was nuts. And the roar of lions, and the screech of apes, and flame-throwers and giants and chicken-gobbling geeks—all were there in my whirligig mind, what used to be me but was now another, unsure as a savage in a new pair of shoes.

How ever could I have known what lay waiting in that schoolboy's hair when I tore it from his head, some strange force roused from its slumber to compel me to Judy with her curlers and dye and leave me, as I'd learn, with powers beyond all doubt?

Before me lay a sea of faces.

Behind stood a wall of mist.

I was afraid of the crowd, but more afraid yet of the solitude I'd left, was beginning to leave, had been so long controlled by.

There were men on the moon, weren't there, taking pictures, collecting stones, leaving their human prints?

I had to be like that, I knew, couragewise, hungerwise, not the print but the foot that made it, a foot even, maybe, that someone could rub at night, perhaps even kiss and lick.

My clothes I'd placed in the closet and drawers. There was nothing to stop me but a view and a door.

There were naked children here, with their naked moms and dads. This was a wholesome place, a world, it seemed, absent ogling sin.

If I wanted to change, I saw, I'd need to bend with the water and bend with the wind, and give of myself in a selfless way.

Frightened, but now not so afraid, I stepped into the sun.

I found Jack by the pool, tense at his umbrella, swatting gnats from his hooch as he listened with dread to Brother Jomar Links wow Jack's "cousin," The Ecdysiast.

Of course he was naked when we met him in the swirl of fun—a fat man splashing ladies with cannonballs off the board, a peck of adolescents playing cribbage in the sun, those two grannies at their yoga, and that dog, even, barking at the raven and the foil in its beak—with rings in his nipples and a tattoo of Jesus on his chest.

Ordained at four, this outlaw from the revivalist school of evangelism had made $300,000 a year preaching to the fallen in churches and tents. His name was "Jomar, Child of Miracles and Joy."

He ran weddings at five, handled serpents at six, and by eight had healed the crippled and lame.

When he did well, he told us, his blue eyes gleaming, his parents bought him such toys as erector sets. When he failed, they smothered him with pillows or held his head in buckets of watery ice.

His father had pedaled Watkins liniment till Jomar was old enough to preach, which he did every Sunday, never once missing a sermon despite his bouts with chickenpox and mumps, accidents on shiny bikes.

His mother smeared his face with makeup and fed him iodine water mixed with vinegar and salt. He drank lots of lemon tea.

"Now *she* was a very unhappy lady," he said, "though she's paid for what she did."

His father left when the boy was twelve, with every cent he'd made—by his account three million bucks, at least.

At sixteen, Jomar ran off, too. He sold canes to blue-haired ladies and called races on the boardwalk, all while playing in a band called The Rictus.

By twenty-two, he'd returned to the circuit with an anti-war pitch that earned him 400 clams a shot. Like Cortez, he said, who'd burned his boats so he couldn't go back, he did an exposé of evangelists, and a rock album, on top of that. Handsome as sin, the man had mistresses from Frisco to Miami.

"I'd fly them in," he said, "and put them at whichever joint the God heads weren't. Then I'd wait till midnight and funk on down to her room, no probs. Sneaking back was a cinch."

He was on the Merv Griffin Show, he was on with Johnny Carson, and they wrote him up in *Playboy* and *Rolling Stone*.

Today, just a few years later, he'd once and for all quit that "scene" to become what he called a "naturist."

"Rachel-baby!" Jack said with some zeal, now, having seen me approach without my clothes. "I can't believe you did it."

"I've been called many things, you guys, but 'killjoy' isn't one of them."

"*Rachel?*" The Ecdysiast said.

I nodded toward Jomar. "Who's your friend?"

"Brother Jomar Links," said the dodger, and rose to take my hand. "Freedom fighter, apostle, born-again naturist, great God almighty. But please, foxy lady, just call me Jomar."

"En*chant*ed," I said.

"And from whom, may I ask," he said like some patriarch of the South, "do I take such *groovy* pleasure?"

"Why," I said in kind, "I'm just little old Rachel Hill. Widow, you know, teacher, sparetime *her*petologist."

Jomar laughed and shook his head while Jack kept up his stare.

"She's Jacky's roommate," The Ecdysiast said. "Would you believe this is her first time in the *nude*?"

"And I'm the man in the moon," Jomar said. "Come on now, Star Child, check me out."

It was plain as a bank this wasn't a call the man had often to make. He had the blarney of a con and shine of the sun, and looked like an angelic Camel Man. We were *checking him out*, all right.

But as for Jack, let me say. He had the biggest penis I'd heard of or seen, maybe the biggest the world had seen, more than a foot long in its, what, *natural state*.

He hauled it up and flopped it on his thigh, better to cross his legs.

Even the regulars here seemed to pause to jaw at the thing, especially when he performed little acts of wonder such as that. Which in my opinion was entirely justifiable. It's not often you get to see a man *literally bodily* move his penis from the inside to the outside of his thigh. Pants or no, it was a distraction, too, from his face mostly, which was definitely a pro—the man had a birthmark on his jaw the color of dirty wine. But now he laid it down with an air of struggle and sighed.

"Groove on it, brother," he said to Jomar while a woman in a visor gawked from the pool. "She's never even worn like a *bath*ing suit."

"One of the reasons I quit," Jomar said, flashing his teeth my way.

He would talk, and you'd listen, and no one would say why. The man swayed the world with words, and the world understood.

"That jive was simple," he said, "as ladies like her putting their hands in my lap in a car or something, all these foxy ladies everywhere. Cause I saw them getting busted, preachers of the gospel, just like me. Even though it's all over the circuit, totally evident. Sex, I mean. Seems like I myself was almost always out of state, you know, I mean like standing above this valley full of bodacious foxes. You dig what I'm saying? Cause I wasn't just supposed to not have a chick or something like that. I was supposed to be, you know, like celibate. Can you imagine what it's like to hear some of the stories these chicks would tell in the prayer lines, and me a healthy young dude all with a young dude's joneses?"

He knew we were listening. His pause was merely a gesture, something, as close as I could put it, resembling a beggar's attempt at *noblesse oblige*.

"Well," he said, "you ladies are pretty funky, I guess, so maybe you can. But I did hear some tales. Like the day that lady came up at the end of the service, a real live one, man, even with her antique beehive and such, and said, *O Brother Jomar, thank you so much for what you've done. While you were preaching, God gave me the most beautiful vision. You were moving like a beautiful lion. And I looked over and saw a little lamb. And I was the little lamb. And now I know you know, Brother Jomar,* this lady says as she takes my hand, *I know you know it says in the Bible that the lion's supposed to lay down beside the lamb.* Well," Jomar said, "I had to tell her. *That,* I told her, *must've been a wondrous vision you had, sister, an inspiration to us all. And as soon as the good Lord finds it in his heart to give me one of the same, I'll be sure to let you know.* Now you get a chick like *that* on the scene," Jomar said, "and I guarantee you'll get busted out of the circuit faster than you can slap me five."

The man sipped his drink, finally.

"But you hear what I'm saying?" he said, looking at The Ecdysiast with bedroom eyes. "I mean, that was always my trip, I guess. I just really dig ladies' bodies."

The Ecdysiast put her hair in a bun and removed her choker. Probably she'd made the blight herself in a macramé class at the Night School for Hippies, what Jack would say was *groovy*.

"I've been waiting *so* long to get out in this sun?" she said. "Gosh, Jo Jo, just think. Pretty soon I'll be almost as tan as *you*."

"Hey, man," Jomar said to Jack in his shade, "when're you going to get with the program? You don't hurry up and catch some rays, summer'll be over and there you'll be, white as a sad old elephant!"

Merle Frizzel had come to our cottage to introduce himself when we arrived. The sight of him through the window with his little belly and kinky hair was unforgettable. And not only was his penis uncircumcised, but he was wearing Roman sandals and holding a plate of hotdogs. Still, I thought, there was something alluring about the man—his shining grin, perhaps, or perhaps his carriage, the sure but sleepy tilt of his head.

"Yes?" I had said.

He looked surprised to see me dressed, though only for a moment.

"Let me guess," he said. "You haven't been, how do they say, *initiated*."

"Pardon?"

He seemed suddenly to realize he wasn't your typical salesman pitching a wife on Elm Street.

"Am I a cluck or what?" he said, and looked over his shoulder. "I kind of just forgot there isn't anyone here for a proper manners making. Fact is, I saw you folks check in and figured you must be new." He bobbed a little, then

35

kicked a rock like a kid. "Anyways, I'm Merle." There was music somewhere, Joan Baez, I thought. Merle extended the plate. "We've got a barbecue happening," he said, "over at the Wagon."

"Thanks, but I'm not all that hungry."

"Nothing strange about that," Merle said with a wink. "Newcomers are pretty often a little rattled."

I stepped from behind the door, still fully clothed, before a naked man, one, actually, who seemed all the more so for his sandals. And yet he had the air of a king. What right did he have to be so persuasively charming? It was I who was vulnerable, *me*.

"It's true," I said. "I've never done this before."

"The important thing is you're here."

"But I don't know where to start."

"Look at it this way. You've already let your hair down."

I'd forgotten about my new do. I felt ridiculous. And now that I'd moved into the open, I had nowhere to hide, or thought I hadn't. Because Merle set his plate on a stone by the door, and with two simple words made me feel as though nothing I'd known was real.

"It's lovely," he said.

I looked into his eyes. "Would you like to come in?"

"This here is a beautiful place you found," he said. "Consider yourself one of the golden few."

It seemed like I was smiling then, I mean really, sincerely *smiling*, for the first time in endless years. I doffed my glasses and stepped inside.

"There'll be time enough for *that*," Merle said, and turned away. At the end of the path, over his shoulder, he said, "I only just wanted to offer, you know, a kind of salutation. You can keep those hotdogs."

"I'm Rachel," I told him. "Rachel Hill."

"I know," he said. "Merle Frizzel. You can't find me, just ask."

And he was no less generous now than when we'd met—like I'd known he'd wanted to be, like I'd wanted him to be. He was looking at me, too, at—wow—but all of me.

"Afternoon, folks," he said.

"Thanks for the hotdogs," I told him, and winked. "I got hungry after all."

"I have to say, Rachel," he said, "seriously, you look— what's the expression?—out of this world."

It struck me as I took his hand that he was the only black man in sight, the only black *hu*man even, in the whole of Freedom Lake. There wasn't so much as another soul you could call even red or brown.

"The gangsta-*lean*," Jomar said, fingers in a V.

"Jomar," Merle said. "*All* right."

"Yeah, man. And will you absolutely *dig* these chicks? Moses on the mountain but are they *hea*vy."

"Me and Rachel," Merle said, his gaze wavering between Jack and The Ecdysiast, "have already more or less had what you might call, you know, a prologue."

You'd think it hard for a man with a penis as big as Jack's to sulk, but he was doing one heck of a job. It was only when Merle held out his hand that Jack began to realize Merle might have stopped to see someone other than Jomar. The best Jack could do was to take Merle by his fingers.

"I made a kind of little trek, I guess," Merle said.

"You know, over your way, but it looks like I missed you. Merle Frizzel."

"Right on, man, it's cool," Jack said, and that was all.

"Hey, Merle," Jomar said, "dig. This here little fox is Jenny."

"Super," Merle said, intimating a bow. "Really a pleasure."

"She's my cousin," Jack said as he looked at me.

"Is that so, is it?" Merle said, helpless now and then to keep from glancing at Jack's incredible appendage.

"Bet you'll never dig what she is," Jomar said. Merle shook his head. "Go on, brother, take a poke. For the sweet baby J."

Merle was just that cute. With his roman sandals and round little belly, he feigned a struggle to guess what it was The Ecdysiast did to make it so worthy of mention.

To my eye, she herself was nigh on writhing in that way of hers, though to the rest she had to've been merely gazing from her lounge, dreamily oceanic. But you could tell just the same that even something so simple as lying in the sun was for her a show. It was as if she'd been trained in indolence, in how to seethe with the promise of a night between her legs, to percolate the notion through her every pore, *ooooohh, ahhhh, oh yes, baby, ooooohh, aaahh?* My God, was she a load.

"The problem, you know, as I see it," Merle said, "my not being able to guess and such, has something to do with the idea that a glamour-type gal all so set as you and everything shouldn't have to lift a finger, which I know may be presumptuous, though it's not, but it's the best I can do."

"You dig that?" Jomar said. "This cat always knows

the right words to say. The golden touch, man, Midas can't hold a flame!" He turned to The Ecdysiast. "Go on, Jenny, lay it on him."

The woman tilted back her head and batted her, what, her I-know-you'd-love-to-love-me eyes. "I don't suppose," she said, "you've ever heard of an Ec*dys*iast?"

"Wow," Merle said, chuckling. "I don't mean any harm, it's nothing personal I hope you know, but that sounds like something I might have to *worry* about."

Now we all laughed, everyone but *my little Jack of Hearts*, as his mother was so fond of saying.

The Ecdysiast, meanwhile, had settled down, waiting for us to follow. To this point, she'd only been Jack's "cousin"—a girl named Jenny first, an intolerable nuisance second, stereotypically beautiful and ditzy, nitwittedly carnal, scheming even, in her way, if a moron can be said to scheme.

Or so at least she seemed. The fancy name for her profession should've been hint enough, because all at once, with the eloquence of a scholar, the woman begat a treatise on the art and history of erotic dance.

"H.L. Menken," she said, scratching lightly at a nipple, "was a writer back in the '20s and '30s, known mostly for his fan*tas*tic wit? Well, anyway, Georgia Sothern, who incidentally is one of my most super idols, was an artist who wanted a more dignified word for her profession, well, she went to him and asked that he come up with something, and he said how about ec*dys*iast? Essentially it's zoo*lo*gical. Apparently from the term *ecdysis,* which I guess has to do with like the act of shedding or molting

39

an outer skin, and that comes from the Greek *ekdyein*, which means, you know, to take or strip off?"

It was astounding.

Had you asked her where electricity's from, she'd have said the switch. Had you asked the difference between night and day, she'd have said, *That's easy, night is when I dance?* And for her a monkey was Davy Jones or Peter Tork.

But where in chit-chat she had the brains of a radish, she was encyclopedic in everything "work." From Carol Doda and Salome to Bettie Page and La Goulue, she knew them to the bone. She knew their times, their places, their dances, their charms. She knew their women and their men, their vices and woes, and could recite any minor scrap of it without a second thought.

She considered, for example, the art of belly dancing sacred as the Hindus their cow and believed the scorn it had suffered in such countries as Egypt and Iran to be the product not so much of religious promulgations as of those whose roots were phallic.

Why, she asked, would men not look the hypocrites they were when they couldn't keep their pants zipped up anytime a woman danced?

"Really," she said, "you know, it's sort of just like H.M. Alexander's book, what the title gets at, you know, the vanished art of burlesque? I mean, if you just think about where it all *started*. There's all sorts of fights and stuff about who it was that invented the art, and nobody's really right or wrong because basically no single performer invented it. It was more like an *evolution* I guess you could say?

"Like Miss Vivian will tell you it was an accident, for instance, you know, that a chorus girl's strap *broke* one night. Ann Corio, though, says Hinda Wausau started it by wearing one costume over the other and taking them off a piece at a time, all to something like thundering applause? And girls like Truly Shattuck and Dainty Marie, and this is like around 1912 or so, plus Millie De Leon, in '15, in St. Louis, I think, who stripped the ruffles off her gown *really, really* slowly? I mean that is *so* cool, that idea, and Edna Maze when she danced to "I Take Off a Little Bit" and ended up in a saucy pair of *black lace trunks*!"

In the distance, out near the line of trees, someone played a trumpet.

Children splashed in the pool, still, though the sun had dipped behind the ridge, and still, too, they were shrieking, certainly enough they had the warmth.

As for The Ecdysiast, she had stunned us into silence. Basically, I think, our approach to the woman had been *what-you-see-is-what-you-get*. She hadn't any more to offer than an eyeful of juice, it appeared, so we'd deemed early on she was your classic nitwit bimbo.

But if there's one thing I've learned, it's that nearly anyone you name is loathe to change their mind about a person known. Garbage men can't talk physics, wisdom says, any more than scientists can jive or strippers think. That The Ecdysiast could do more than gibber and twit, much less expound, was no less fantastic than a baby climbing a wall.

Notwithstanding the feminism that had been cropping up wherever you turned, it was hard enough to find a man who could fathom a pretty woman with more than two ideas.

Ordinarily I wouldn't have counted myself into that bunch, but seeing how The Ecdysiast had already shown her proverbial colors, I had no choice.

And that goes for the rest of them. Not even Jack, I could tell, had been privy to this loquacious aspect of her, what, her *talent*. He'd been reduced, in short, to a slack-jawed cluck with a penis in his hand.

It wasn't, either, like we were listening to the Man of Miracles and Joy. When a preacher opens his mouth, you don't expect him to say, *Will you please pass the ketchup?* or *Mount Fuji is a fluke!* He's going to ramble and exhort, you think, for minutes in the least, or for hours. And you expect to listen, or to convey the impression.

I looked at Jomar's face, spellbound and tense, and wondered if he'd glimpsed the link between his appearance to others—crying out hosannas at the age of four, or healing cripples, or incanting rites for people five times older—between that and The Ecdysiast now, so marvelously earnest in her nudity that the question of her reality had been rendered all but moot.

Surely there was an on-the-tip-of-your-tongue quality to the air, the sense that some imp of disarray and wine was gamboling just beyond the edges of our circle, performing, as it were, its striptease of broken expectations, sure without malice or heat, without judgment, like a child at play by the sea.

The tattooed Jesus on Jomar's chest shimmered with his sweat.

Jack was catatonic.

I was rapt.

Merle alone had remained aloof, and this was understandable. The man had only just met this beautiful surprise. He'd had no chance to see her in other light. He was smiling as he did and bobbing away while The Ecdysiast spun her words.

"I mean, you guys get the point," she said, "right?"

She, too, was sweating, lusciously, almost, even fragrantly. Something had happened. Somehow I'd become smitten by her, somehow I'd become endeared.

Because if you stopped to consider, there wasn't much light between us.

Just the day before, I thought, not without irony, I'd asked to be turned into a Zeigfeld girl, a dancer, namely, in spirit, at worst. The Ecdysiast and I were two of a kind, I saw, commensurate as twins—if being obsessed with one ideal counted, if loneliness or tenderness counted, the tiniest spot of hope.

"Well *of course* we do," I said. "Go on, go on."

"Super!" The Ecdysiast said.

The creature was so bright she couldn't cast a shadow.

"But so what got me started I guess was how I really meant to say about how striptease isn't what it used to be. I mean I guess you could say that's why I do it? To, I don't know, kind of take it back, you know, reclaim whatever kind of glory it might once have had.

"Really, my thing, what I'm *going* for, is sort of in between something like what La Goulue did at the Moulin *Rouge*, you know, the cahut and that sort of thing, and then

43

like the stuff Georgia Sothern did, her, Rosita Royce, and maybe Lili St. *Cyr*, plus like a liberal dose, too, of course of Isadora Duncan and Loie Fuller? There wouldn't be a snatchy thing about it. Nothing even hardly filthy or shameful, not like that *crab* Bettie Page, you know, I don't even know why they go in for her the way they do, I mean if only they really knew where she's been, I can tell you. That smile? It's like frozen and stuff, like you know, all distorted even. *God*.

"Really what I want to do, I guess, and then I'll stop talking, is mostly take the art back from all the double-d retards and stuff who've made it practically nothing but a big old joke for men with milk bottles and raw liver and stuff, I mean because that's the kind of stuff they bring in there you know, I swear to God, and anyhow, you know, take it back and just like give it some *real* meaning, some real *feeling* and even hopefully some respect. Seriously, isn't that all anybody ever wants for doing something that means something really im*por*tant to them and probably a whole lot of *others*?"

The sun was still shining, the birds still singing and bees all buzzing, and we were wholly stunned.

Jomar, astonished, passed an eye round us all and downed the rest of his drink. "Whoa, man! What do you cats think?"

"Heck," Merle said. "I only came over to invite you folks to a game of ping-pong, and then this, I don't even know what to call it, it was so fantastic—this *gift*."

"You said it, Midnight," Jomar said. His teeth were bright, his skin as gold as gold. "That was just about the heaviest load of mindblow I've heard in *years*, man! I've got to give it to you," he said to The Ecdysiast. "That was *primo*."

The Ecdysiast, I forgot to say, had by the end of her speech been reduced to tears. There was no doubt to her sincerity—the sincerity, I thought, of some remarkably corrupt Madonna.

I imagined her at work.

She'd appear on stage in tenebrous glow, her nipples with their tassels veiled by silk. The voice of Bas Sheva would accompany her, lusty and scathing, husky, soaring, swooping, arcing, and The Ecdysiast would move to the subtlety of that call while trumpets, bongos, and flutes wove in and out of one voodoo nuance after the next, theremins, too, spooky with the full-moon choir, a savagely woven movement of caterwauling beasts, all of it a single voice there to make The Ecdysiast the aural jungle through which to trail the dust of her terpsichorean magic.

There would be incense.

There would be smoke.

She'd be sinuous as Tisiphone, the boa in my class at school, this flourish lingering, that wave tarrying, undulation after heated undulation.

And the audience would murmur, and sighs would throb and melt.

And meanwhile her garments would drift, underpants, slippers, veils, but still the wrap would stay, billowing, enough to glimpse the skin golden at her breast, the branch of her loins, that bit of buttock or glistening nape, telling without divulging, maintaining, as it were, the integrity of her charm, since, like a flower shorn of petals, what is revelation but the edge of death, the secret, finally and at last, plundered and gored and spilled?

Those in attendance, men and women both, would sense, if not know, the greatness of her aim, its absence of any *self*. This would be her *raison d'etre*, the whole of her tireless ambition. How could it not?

A person sings the praises of her calling, resolves into tears for and by it, longs for its transcendence without regard for anything else, and how could you believe she was somehow not a saint?

Her performance would be an act of piety so full of selfless ardor that the emotions it provoked couldn't but be commuted to a bog of dismay, and this because, first, you'd know that sooner or later it had to end, and, second, especially, because you yourself could never sacrifice enough for such a tribute, the total giving of yourself for an idea without thought of gain or praise.

I couldn't merely admit it. I had to bow down before it: in every possible way, The Ecdysiast had outdone the folly of public reason.

There in the face of that suite of unfeigned hallelujahs, this realization, for all of us, I thought, constituted one of those moments that, like an assassin, creeps up and takes you. Only afterward do you understand the profundity of what's passed. We'd been left, as it were, screwy-eyed and helpless, slowly to gurgle on the blood from the gashes at our throats.

"You ought not to listen to them," I told her, and winked at Merle. "It's quite obvious," I said, "that they're scarcely more than philistines."

"So, Rachel," Jack said.

I'd nearly forgotten about him, he'd been so quiet on his chaise lounge in the shade. The rest, broad in the sun and sweating for old Beelzebub himself, had overlooked him, too, it seemed. In formation, we turned his way. He'd let go his penis and leaned in like a heckler.

"Since when," he said, "did you decide to get all uppity and shit? I mean, cause in case you were wondering, Jenny makes more money in a week than you do in like half a year."

"Excuse me, *friend*," Merle said. "Pardon me. Not to put too fine a point on it, but I'm mostly pretty sure, and of course I could be wrong you know, I've been known to be wrong a whole bunch of times actually, but like I was saying, I'm pretty certain Rachel was only *joking*. Right?" he said, and looked into my eyes.

The Ecdysiast seized my hand. "That was so nice of you, Rachel. I mean, I can tell, you know, that you totally understand where I'm coming from?"

"Maybe I was wrong, too," Jomar said to Jack. "About what I said back then about you needing to get some sun."

"Lay it on me, brother," Jack said coldly.

"It's just that you seem like maybe you're a little *zoned* there already. You know, kind of fried like."

Jack stared hard at Jomar. "Dude, I'm totally mellow."

"Whatever it is you've been taking, man, do me a favor and keep it to yourself?"

"*People*," Merle said. "I was wondering. Is there even the slightest possibility that in all this excitement my offer maybe got, how would you say it, slightly *disregarded*?"

"I'm *so* sorry," The Ecdysiast said. "What did you say?"

"*Ping-pong*," Merle said, and swung a hand. "I mean, talk about working the old gluteus maximus. Folks don't know it, but there's an awful lot of lunging goes on in a good game of ping-pong. Very good for the ladies, especially, for their figures I mean, if that's not stepping too far out of line."

He looked at Jack, and then at Jack's penis, and put his hands before him.

"Stay calm now, okay, we're all friends here, right, and yeah, well, I'd really appreciate it if you didn't leap up to club me with that thing."

Who knows what in Merle's joke brought the fire out of Jack, but then and there he bolted from his lounge to gyrate like a guy with a hula hoop. In no time at all his penis had gathered so much drive we could've called it a propeller.

"The helicopter!" Jack shouted. "Come on, everybody! Let's do the helicopter!"

There was a jiffy of silence—we of course were shocked—and then, at once, a burst of extreme laughter.

"Somebody best hurry up and grab that cat," Jomar said. "He's so far out he's about to disappear!"

And so there it was—the pimple on the pretty baby's bottom. Leave it to my little Jack of Hearts. The man had a way with things, that's for sure.

Ping-pong in the gloaming, flit and bounce of the little white ball, and breasts that jiggled, and phalli that dangled, and mouths of laughter, mouths of jest, peals and squeals and yawping.

We were drunk.

Or they were drunk, in any case, The Ecdysiast, Jomar, and Jack.

I had to comport myself. I needed, as it goes, all the *sangfroid* I could get.

The grounds had thinned, the children were hungry, their parents happily worn. Odor of chicken, odor of ribs, and hotdogs and steaks, and shish kabobs and beans and corn on the cob, these were on the air, a freshly issuing jasmine, too, mingling with the tune of hidden birds.

Much lunging indeed—Merle had not embroidered.

Nor was he drunk, either. In fact, from what I could see, he hadn't had a nip. He was a sprightly man, of vigor and joy, and for all his clumsiness at ping-pong itself—it's true, it's true, he was terrible—I have to say he was a pleasure to watch, if not an inspiration.

Not to mention he'd somehow got Jomar and Jack to form a team against The Ecdysiast and himself. He had compelled them, in other words, with perfect gentility, to cooperate and compromise. By the time they'd made it halfway through, those two cads were ribbing their opponents with good-natured mockery, slapping each other five.

"There's a certain special kind of something to ping-pong," Merle said. "A sort of, you know, anti-swagger, if that's the word."

He was heaving like a laborer, smiling, as if satisfied with the near-critical scope of his fatigue.

"That's because ping-pong, I guess, if you stop to think about it, no exaggeration, is mostly all about Zen."

"Dude," Jack said, "you're the worst ping-pong player I've ever seen."

"*God, Jacky*," The Ecdysiast said. "I didn't know you could be so mean?"

"I'm just about more horrible than he is, so I can talk."

"Cat's so heavy," Jomar said, nodding at Merle, "he's been trying to move that ball with his *mind*."

"No," Merle said. "I mean, maybe there's a chance you guys don't see my gist. It's more like an *at*titude. I mean, the ball just keeps coming back, right? And, well, when it doesn't, you go and pick it up."

"Amen to that!"

"I think this is all just so *real*," The Ecdysiast said. "I mean, you know, Merle, you're totally right on, I think, even if I'm not real sure what you're actually talking about."

There was a bowl of fruit on the table. Merle peeled a banana, then bit it.

"*That*," he said, "is what I'm talking about."

"Now you're beginning to freak even *me* out," Jomar said.

"Same as ping-pong," Merle said. "It's *Zen*."

"Bananas are my absolutely most favorite fruit?" The Ecdysiast said.

"The man freaked like *this*," Jomar said, "in some of the congregations I've worked, and they'd have him on a stake faster than you can take off your clothes."

"Eating a banana?" Jack said. "That's *heavy*?"

Merle held up the rest of the banana. "Step over here," he told Jack. Jack did, and Merle waved the fruit beneath Jack's nose. "And *this*," Merle said, his face beatific with a soft half-smile.

"What the flippety-floo are you talking about?" Jomar said.

"I have to put it all in words," Merle said, "I'd be committing something along the lines of blasphemy. It's pretty much the last resort for any self-respecting monk, you know, to have to go and actually say what Zen is, even though there's no such thing as blasphemy in Zen, not really, which again isn't to say it's related to Satanism or anything, don't get me wrong, but anyway, if I do have to put it in words, which by the looks of it is what you guys are making me, you could say *Zen is an elephant doing a flea*."

Jack set down his paddle and picked up the last of his doobie.

"I just want to forget the static," he said, "you know, all the hassle? Cause I mean if gobbling down a banana is Zen, then copping a killer-ass hit has got to be *triple* Zen. At least try it sometime, dude. Maybe you'll feel better."

He turned to the rest of us. "What do you boners say we spark up the fondue? I'm totally ravenous."

It was all so unbelievable, all so, what, unexpected. So much so, in fact, that suddenly I realized nothing about this place would surprise me.

And yet once again I was mistaken.

From out of the collapsing dusk a man strode toward us hand in hand with a woman who might've been an apple tainted by the sun.

They were, I'd learn, the drug-addled swingers from Amsterdam, Wolfgang and Usch, famous at Camp Freedom Lake, and as old.

"You are all waiting for this things to happen, yes?" Wolfgang said with not the slightest fanfare. He was talking, I believed, to me. "In the common," he said, "we are dressed more airy when we are not here so that is nice that no people are forcing now, and so it must also be in view that we are plainly happy."

"Yes," Usch said, "we are just continue our stroll."

"Yes," Wolfgang said proudly as one hand hugged his disproportionate testicles, "our erotical stroll."

Though she'd done nothing to warrant the sense, the woman seemed unusually vivacious for her age, late-sixties, perhaps, or perhaps early seventies, a year or two older than Wolfgang, I guessed, if not five or six. And, despite the faint silliness of the ragged bangs of her pageboy coif and her giant ears virtually aflap, she was in charge, that for sure was clear.

"This nights," she said, gesturing at large to the fuzz all around, "is so beautiful for this things to happen, for all this lovely *things*!"

I watched her with a garbled horror that, when she leaned in to pet my hair, birthed as a sound I'd never made, between the cry of a rabbit and coo of a sated lover.

Adrenaline coursed through me, my eyes felt radically large.

This wasn't some heinous crime that had just obtained, and yet, like a fly in sap, I stayed, immobile with trepidation.

I'd always thought so, and so I thought now: fear is a gremlin in the drain, waiting for you to forget it was you who flushed it down.

"You are *R*achel is that so?" Usch said.

My state at this point far overshot a thing like panic. I couldn't twitch, much less move.

When finally an imperceptible nod wound its way to my skull, Usch bared her teeth and said, "Yes. We have listened to many things in these talkings, you know. Your hairs. *They are noticed.*"

O Abel Rich, you little spawn from hell, where were you now?

Whatever were you doing, young devil, and when would you leave me be?

Enough!

I knew where he was. He was there, right there, a germ in my heart, and there, in the shadows before me, a bisexual swinger with a twitch in her eye and a penchant for quiet malice.

I lay back and watched her arms expand like wings.

"*Wel*come, Merle!" she said.

"Welcome to *you*, Usch," Merle said, and passed a quick but sensitive glance my way before taking her hand to kiss it. It was a glance that said, *Do as I do, but above all, beware.* "And to you also, Wolfgang," he said. "It's a beautiful place we've found, I think, we're all very fortunate, some of the golden few."

"Are not these the moment," Usch said, "that you always mostly enjoy? And all of you as well," she said, gazing round our faces.

"Forget about your moments," Jack said. "We want to see your *things*. Where's all these *things* you've been blabbing about is what we want to know."

"This peoples, Merle," Wolfgang said. He was moving through us, touching us one by one—Jomar's chest, The Ecdysiast's arm, Jack's rangy hairless buttocks. "How have you come to them all on yourself?"

"Probably," The Ecdysiast said, "he *drove*? I mean but there's always the real chance, too, that he flew here just like Jo Jo did. Some people are just totally lucky?"

"The cat," Jomar said, nodding at Merle, "is a magician of the *so*ciogenial-type. Covers ground like a cosmic field of snow. Do I *lie*, Snowflake," he said, and slapped Merle's shoulder, "or do I *lie*?"

Merle was on the verge of responding when Usch cut him off. "*Ma*gic, yes," she said. "That is *wo*rthy. Each peoples knows this kind of games, with those *ma*gic, but not each body knows this kind that is erotical."

"Oh but you're wrong about that, foxy lady," Jomar said. He tapped his chest. "This here freek can play any game on the list, the heavier the better, I always say."

"And this *ta*ttoos that you have, of this *Je*sus fellows," Wolfgang said, so fond of his body, as we and the blind could plainly see. He was massaging, now, his rather icky paunch. "Why can you do anythings erotical with that?"

Jack lit up another of the doobies I bought him, then gave Jomar a nudge and whispered. "Where'd these kooks say they tripped in from again?"

"They got you strung out with some bad vibes, hey, brother?"

Jomar tapped his chest once more and spoke at the swingers like that phony southern patriarch.

"I shall now inquire of you good people," he said, "and, please, don't go into any of that funny stuff revolution business here when you answer. What was my good man JC if not the world's greatest lover?"

"Hey you, *Jesus* man," Usch said. "We are not this hippies, yes? We are *erotical*!"

Jomar laughed. We all did.

"All this things that are beautiful," Wolfgang said, "are even most better when they are with a spot of *other* good things," he said, smiling very lasciviously, I thought. "Usch got very *hungry* sometime with this good *things* that she take. All of you peoples should like some of this things, especially, I start to think, this very beautiful womans there with all this beautiful *hairs*."

The Ecdysiast, of course, was about to accept this compliment with her naive aplomb, but Wolfgang, like his wife, grabbed my hair. Unlike his wife, however, he didn't paw or even stroke it, but simply held it. The Ecdysiast, meanwhile, aware of her blunder, paused, her ambiguous hand dangling in the dark.

I was ensnared between the need to swat Wolfgang's

fingers from my head and my fascination with The Ecdysiast. She looked so vulnerable, so indistinct, there in the mounting darkness, a little like a girl, I thought, caught in the act of wetting herself.

But the sense was fleeting.

With a toss of her golden locks she said now was the time, she could wait no more, the lily gods were calling, she said, she had to obey, it was, she said, like real hard not to. And then she rose to the tips of her drunken toes and performed a pirouette, and then again rushed away with flapping arms.

Wolfgang, blast him, still had my hair, rubbing it like a bit of silk.

"So, Wolfgang," Merle said.

"Mr. *Mag*ic, is this a troubles that you cannot see?" Wolfgang said.

"What are you hiding there," Merle said, squinting at Wolfgang's hand, "or putting there in Rachel's hair, or maybe you're looking for something, or what?"

"This *hairs*," Wolfgang said. He was staring at my hair now with a look so glazed it could only have signified weird intent. "What *are* these? They are not any hairs that I have known. Usch," he said, looking up with his druggy eyes. "This *hairs*."

"Yes," Usch said. "They are *noticed*."

"Let me see," Merle said, and took the hair from Wolfgang.

At the same time, quite cleverly, I thought, Merle laid a hand on my back. He had his excuse: he needed me for ballast to examine my hair. But actually he'd allowed his weight to settle on the leg nearest mine.

His hand on my thigh was plain to see—the fingers at my back were not.

After so many days of neglect, this touch, and the coolness of it, abruptly contextualized my snag: not till now had I known how hot I was, how badly I'd been burned.

That I was surprised by this was doubtless its own surprise. What, after all, had I expected?

Most of my life had been spent in the dark. I'd never had more color than the belly of a frog.

A shiver swept through me, then, I was hot, then cold, then hot again and cold, and a mild nausea stirred my bowels. My muscles were knit. I was feverish and very, very stiff.

"Looks to me, Wolfie," Merle said, and winked like he did, "that you've been the victim of an angel in disguise. There's nothing here but a headful of gorgeous hair."

Even as Merle spoke, I could feel Jack's gaze. There was that same speck of hatred in his eye, that same sure look of impotent rage. He stood up, his giant penis looming, and—pretty comical, I had to say—actually sneered.

"It's like one day she's got this big-ass Uncle Sam hairdo," he said, "and the next she comes home looking like some rich honky momma off a cruise ship."

My warm chaise of gold might well have become a black couch of sorrow at this bitty malfeasance, but reality, thank God, is grey. Jack was Jack. Nastiness, stupidity, greed—these foibles of his were the foibles of all and so merely more noise in the rush of the same that's the world.

The Ecdysiast was shouting, the waters were laughing. From a nearby copse a kid cried out, *Ollie ollie oxen free!*

A chorus of cricketsong and batsong had begun to mount, and moths were at the torches and lights.

And if that weren't enough, Usch had commenced to tromp out a tune distinctly Wagnerian.

Dun da-da dun dun! Dun da-da dun dun!

No wonder, I thought, because, yes, it really was Wagner, doubtless as an infant, no wonder at all, since, remember, the woman wasn't just Dutch but like the phantom of her tune as carnal and mad as a dog of the sea.

There was a creepy air of déjà vu to the business, of concatenation tainted, what I couldn't define or see but somehow knew, the way you know you're being watched from a hedge in a park.

Jomar, coward that he was, had used this spat to drift to the edge of our circle, headed, I well knew, toward The Ecdysiast in her pool. I alone had heard Jack's words, though I didn't say.

One by one, we were yielding to this screwball night.

"It sounds like she might be drowning over there," I said to Jomar as soon as he'd ventured far enough off for us to see his intent. "You'd best go *save* her."

"I heard that," Jomar said, and vanished. Another minute later we heard, "Praise the lord, Sugarmouth! It's Jomar, Child of Miracles and Joy, here to sock it to you!"

"Yeah, well," Jack said, glancing toward the pool, as if there were a relationship between it and his words, "you can't go dancing in a broom closet, and one monkey sure don't stop no show."

He'd scarcely spoken before Wolfgang, his lips a snarl of revelation, began to holler.

"Usch!" he said. "I know why now that this hairs have all been *noticed*!" He hadn't for an instant ceased to stare at my locks. "It is their goldenness, yes, that it is more unthinkable, do you see, the color that they are, like a sun!"

Yet another chill swept across me.

I needed something then, that much I knew, a pill perhaps, or maybe just a snappy drink.

Ecstatic, like rapists in an alley, almost, the Hollanders were closing in, their teeth dully glinting. And now Jack, too, had slunk toward the pool.

"I'm not feeling so well," I told Merle. "I think maybe I've been burned."

"What?" he said, and retreated. My arm was the color of pig's feet, pickled, the kind you see on counters in country stores. "Burned?" he said. "*Oh*," he said. "Yeah, I mean, oh boy, stupid old me, I guess it's pretty obvious now that you think about it. I mean it's been so long and all, what with, well, you know, it seems like I haven't worn a *shirt* in years."

He was so cute, the way he stammered and blinked with his belly and sandals and twinkling eyes, I could hardly stand it.

"It's okay," I said.

"She is not feeling robust from this suns?" Wolfgang said.

The best word to describe this man, I thought, was *crestfallen*.

"Mr. *Ma*gic, hey," Usch said. "Is this the corrections?"

"Kind of looks that way," Merle said.

"From all of this suns then, yes?"

"Yep."

Wolfgang's face had lightened again. "This mans," he said to Usch. "Do you remember, the one who come every year in the ends of the summer with all this erotical womans each time, remember, until when he died from these hearts he had?"

"Oh, yes," Usch said. "*Very* erotical womans he had. And all this good things also."

"There was no peoples like him for the sun until now," Wolfgang said.

He reached out and lightly poked my calf. A sulfurous moon appeared where his finger had been, and then a burst of pink.

"Yes," he said. "I see. Like this, the beginning days or two this mans always did not look so well. Very white, then very pink, and then—*taaa!*—all of these skins was gone and he was very golden, very erotical, yes."

"It was all this things he poured on himself, Wolfie, all this, what did he say, *alla baras.*"

"Aloe vera?" Merle said.

"Yes," Usch said. "This mans, what was the name he called by, yes, that's the things he poured, *aloe vera.*"

"This *names* he had," Wolfgang said. "Was it not something like a Terrence or one of these like that?"

"Yes," Usch said. "Like that, I think it was this."

"No," Wolfgang said. "It was not *this.* This names, now that I am sure, it was *Clarence.* Yes, I remember these very strong now."

"Yes, Wolfie, that is *strong*! That is what he called by! *Clarence!*"

"What?" I said, my insides turned to a roil of bugs.

"This erotical mans with all this pink skins," Wolfgang said. "All this summers we met him here for many erotical moments. He was called by the name of *Clarence*."

The chances that the Clarence these two had known was the Clarence I had known—my dearest, my very, my sadly long-lost Clarence—well, they seemed to me, these chances, here in this heaven of gold, far past comprehension. And yet someway, despite, I sensed the worst, as if against an army of angels an imminent darkness loomed.

"*What?*" I said again.

"Could it be that you *meet* this mans, *R*achel?" Usch said.

"Yes," Wolfgang said, "and these man, *Clar*ence—do you remember, Usch?—he had on his foot an extra toe!"

"Yes!" Usch said. "This was what was true, these little toe he had besides his other toes, like a rotten nut."

Already the thought of Clarence on his trips, selling, as he'd maintained, concessions to campgrounds and parks, had turned the air bitter, filled, I don't know how, with the taste of okra, but at this revelation the world on its axis stuttered and balked, the glitch, surely, before complete disaster.

How could I have been so blind? Had I always been so blind?

"You really could use some lotion," Merle said, sweet man. "Because now I'm looking at you and all, really closely and everything, it's more or less just like you said. You're pretty badly burned." He pursed his lips and shook his head. "*Wow.*"

61

My burn was so bad I was sick.

But as luck would have it, chivalrous Merle walked me to my cabin and stayed by my side till the worst had passed. I was ashamed he should see me, but there was nothing for it. I needed him, caught in the throes of self-pity as I was, woebegone and sad, *boo hoo hoo*. Because no sooner would a spell of vomiting end than I'd collapse in a bout of moans and tears. The vomiting Merle understood. It was the abjection that left him baffled.

This, of course, was to be expected. That he could know that Clarence had been my husband, or that, where so many others had seen something of his nature, I myself had caught not a stitch—who or what he was, or told people he was, or what, even, he appeared to be—this was strictly impossible.

In the end it was fine. Nor was any of this something Merle needed said. His concern was to comfort me, and with that he was so perfect I never saw the panic he'd claimed to feel as I related my dismay in the wake of the Hollanders', what—their *onslaught*, I suppose.

The moment I got that Clarence was the man they'd known—*my* Clarence, my *hus*band—our life together, mine and his, roared through my head like a dirge of bats.

All those windswept midnights telling stories in our bed, for instance, and the time, especially, he told me his tale of the Hand of Glory.

That particular marvel, Clarence had said, is the hand of a man freshly hanged, severed at the wrist and wrapped up tight in a winding sheet. Before the wrapping, however, Clarence said, the hand must be thoroughly squeezed, to ensure it's drained of blood, then pounded with a mix that includes peppercorns, saltpeter, and something known as zimort, then cured in an earthenware jar for fifteen days. It is imperative, Clarence said, that the hand remain sealed for fifteen days, no more, no less, after which it's placed in the hottest sun, preferably when Sirius loped in the daytime sky, though where this wasn't possible a furnace fueled by bracken and vervain would suffice.

"The point," Clarence said, "of this aspect of the preparation will be immediately obvious when I say that you must collect the fat that runs from the hand and mix it with a wax that has itself been mingled with the powdered sperm of the deceased. Ghoulish in the extreme, I know, but necessary. For, you see, this amalgam is imperative to the successful creation of the candle that is to be held by the hand itself, between its devilishly stiffened fingers."

"I'm not sure," I told Clarence, "that I want to hear anymore. It's too horrific, even for me."

"Come now, my dear," he said. "Let us not be mawkish."

"Why this foul detail about the hanged man's seminal fluids? Why this candle, as you call it?"

"That should have been obvious, as I explained. Surely it makes sense that adulterating the wax with the dead man's sperm would imbue it with an onanistically doomed quality, a quality of the accursed? Well, and this, it follows, in conjunction with the lifelessness and bloodlessness of the hand itself, endows the candle with the power to strike any person on whom its light falls as blind and as motionless as the dead—*if*, of course, that is your will."

"How silly of me," I said, having not the faintest idea where my husband was headed. "Still, do me the favor of indulging me for another minute or two and explain the need to commit such an abomination at all?"

"Ah," said Clarence. "That recalls to mind the words of Eliphaz the Temanite to Job in his anguish. *How much more abominable and filthy*, he said, *is man, who drinketh iniquity like water?*"

"Dear husband, really, I'll love you so much the more when you cease to toy with me."

"In the same way that Mallory mounted Everest merely because it was there," Clarence said, "some men will commit evil only because they can. It is almost, I'd venture to say, human nature."

"That," I said, "is debatable."

"Perhaps. But let us proceed. Imagine, if you will, the *power* of the man who wields a Hand of Glory?"

"Or the *woman*," I said.

"Yes. Think of the acts that he, or she, could commit with complete and utter impunity?"

"My God," I said, "yes. Really, I suppose, the list is endless."

"As endless as time," Clarence said.

"If you have a tale to knit," I said, "please do."

And so Clarence went on to say that from as far back as the Middle Ages and right up until recently modern times, we humans have used the Hand of Glory to achieve our nefarious ends.

In the fifteenth century, for example, Petrus Mamoris speaks of people carrying *the Hand of a Corpse unto which the Sacraments hath been applied and with which, over some Sleeper, and in reverséd fashion, they maketh the sign of the Cross, that it might causeth him to lie in profoundest Slumber for whole Days without waking, so that they might rob his House at leisure.*

Almost six-hundred years later, in Brooklyn in 1939, an alliance of poisoners used the Hand of Glory to commit several murders and then collect the life insurance of their victims.

But in this case, whereas the hand in question was real, severed from a corpse and mummified, the gang that used it had dispensed with the stipulated candle and pointed up two fingers like a pair of horns.

Years later, Freddie the Bastard O'Callahan, the gang's ruthless boss, was quoted as saying, *Alls you'd have to do is shove that thing in their faces and they'd shrink back like you was the Prince of Darkness Hisself. I seen them have strokes and mess in their pants even when they seen that hand we had. It was just the ticket for the kind of work we done, all right.*

Clearly these tales were not for all. They were comparable, nevertheless, with those of such fabulators as sweet Dr. Seuss and dear Mother Goose when set beside what Clarence related next.

"There was once a man," he said, "whose love went unrequited for years. He'd tried everything to win his beloved, from serenading her in the moony light to sending her gifts of silver and gold and other shiny things. He fought for her in the streets and recited the poems of Rilke and Neruda from a megaphone in the plaza on Sunday afternoons, and yet the woman remained as impervious to his entreaties as a stone to rain.

"At long last, then, in his despair, the man consulted with a woman known for her wisdom in matters of love and hate. Immediately upon hearing his plight, for it was that obvious, the sibyl determined that the man should never prevail with the aid of some common panacea, nor, in fact, could he begin to approach the remotest chance of success until he'd obtained none other than the one true Hand of Glory. *Forget sweet balms*, the sorceress said, *ointments and salves. Hope not for the miracle of Nepenthe or the oblivion of Lethe. King Mithridate cannot help you, for thou art among the most forlorn of men. And yet beware, too,* she warned, *the Hand of Glory you must, as beneath the aegis of the weak it can work the brightest of miracles or the heaviest of woes.* By then, of course, the man had ceased to hear the sibyl's words. She'd spoken of this diabolical hand. Now he needed merely perform the deeds to acquire it. His love, you see, my dear, was just that strong.

"It began as you might guess, with his inveigling one of the homeless into his dwelling place, where he then hung the man from the pipes in his cellar. According to the sibyl's every letter, he severed the hand, he bled the hand, he pickled and cured and baked it. He followed the instructions perfectly, until at last the hand was complete, and ghastly and grim it was. To employ the Hand upon his lady, though—then would his goal be met! And so that night he crept into her room to wave it above her while incanting, *Non erat amor qui perderetur inter eos! Non erat amor qui perderetur inter eos!*

"Lest I forget, allow me to mention also that prior to embarking upon this wretched endeavor, our man had been assured by the sibyl that his spell once cast would not take for several days. Notwithstanding this assurance, however, when his lady hadn't rushed forth to pronounce her undying love, much less to search him out, the man began to fret. He sweated sleepless in his sheets, he wandered the automotive highways and byways, he smoked one cigarette after the next with never a thought for food. All, yes, for the love of a woman. All because he'd wanted for her to give him her heart, and for her to take his own. These, in fact, had more or less amounted to the words he'd been incessantly repeating. *Give me your heart for a day, beloved,* he'd cried month after month, *and mine shall be yours forever!* But now he'd waited long enough. If in the next day or two his beloved hadn't come to him, he would pray for more tenderness in the sweet by-and-by, then end his prolific misery. Life without love, he'd come to see, *this* life, was life bereft of meaning.

"Then it happened. Suddenly and without warning, there amidst the waffle irons and beaters of the department store, on a Sunday afternoon that in days past would have expired like the breath of an asthmatic child, his beloved appeared before him, her eyes moist with desire and her mouth so evidently yearning that he could no longer doubt his fortune. And it was so. The lady was smitten to the core, his votary of ardor and sweetness come true at last.

"Titans in the blood! Ogres in the heart! Dearest, these expressions were as useless as a cry in a freezer when pressed to make meaningful the couple's desire, for immediately she set her gaze upon him, she began to advance, turkey baster in hand like some great truncheon of love. Indeed, so ravenously eager were they both that had it not been for the nearby fitting room, the citizens fortunate enough to have shared their proximity would've beheld an act of public copulation so violently unmarshaled, so undeniably canine, that it could only have surpassed all others, in any book or history, though it be writ by the hand of one of the masters themselves, Boccaccio, for example, or Aretino or Rochester.

"This consummation was merely a start. As I hoped to

suggest, their love was in the extreme. It was so far beyond the man's expectations, in fact, that he had begun to believe happiness a thing of tawdry obsolescence. Immediately the couple assumed the ways of the anthropophagi—to eating, that is, one another's flesh. At first this occurred during the course of their lovemaking alone, in measures small enough, naturally, to prevent either of them from suffering any real danger, but sufficient to ensure that future days would not leave them unmarred. Considered in lieu of their physical intermingling, this mutual feeding had come to fill them with the sense that they were one eucharistic wafer to the other, so to speak, that, truly, with every successive meal their consecration was that much more sublime. Essentially speaking, what had in the beginning been the natural outcome of fiery eros was now a full-blown diablerie.

"Their obsession, however, couldn't be satisfied by a simple draught of blood here, a morsel of flesh there, or rather, I should say, *hers* could not. Whereas he could at least approach the region of satiation, her own longing was as endless as ferocious. Essentially, the woman rose each day from her exhausted slumber only to begin clawing at her lover's chest, digging, as it were, toward his heart. *I must have it!* she'd cry. *It belongs as much to me as does mine to you! We must give ourselves to one another, completely, O dearest radiance, and then we must die!*

"Needless to say, this unexpected development did not fail to engender in our man a sensation not unlike grievous anxiety. On any given day the man could be sure to awaken beneath the nails of his lady, his chest

71

a veritable wormpot of muscle and flesh, and he did, repeatedly. And nothing he said, and nothing he did, could assuage her.

"Worse and worse his lover grew until, finally, one dark and stormy night, it came to pass that the man found himself submerged in the most hideous of dreams. Through a tenebrous corridor enshrouded with spider webs and roses in decline, his lady, enslimed with gore, advanced zombie-like upon him. He leapt screaming from the bed, only to learn that his vision was not a dream but horrific waking truth. Nearer and nearer his lady drew, and soon he could see that in one outstretched hand she held a dripping knife, while in the other a heart—her own! And then, terror stricken, now, paralyzed to the core, our man saw that, like a bottomless mouth, his lover's breast was rent with a sucking wound.

"And once he'd stared into this wound, our man could not look away. His gaze had been forfeited, he knew, his mind plucked like a nut from a shell. When at last he mustered the wherewithal to wrench his eyes from that eldritch sight, it was too late, for his lover was upon him. *My sweet*, she cried, *I've given you all my love. I've given you my life, I've given you my soul, and here, in total worship, at last I give you my heart itself. But please, my love, I beseech you, before I succumb to hell's grim tyrant, share in my ecstasy and do as have I!* And with that she placed her heart in his hands and plunged her dagger into his chest. A moment later, our man's beloved rose with her trophy, gnawing at it like a beast of carrion. And then in another moment yet, she fell upon him, each of them gorgeously dead.

"Little did the man know," Clarence said, "that it was he himself who'd sealed his destiny when on that fatal night he'd stood above his sleeping lover with the Hand of Glory, speaking the words he believed would make her his. But whereas he should have said, *Ne sit amor quin perdendus inter nos*—'Let there be no love lost between us'—instead in his fever he had whispered, *There was no love to lose between them.* And though he'd not paid heed, recall that he had been warned. *Beware, too, the Hand of Glory you must,* the sibyl had said, *as beneath the aegis of the weak it can work the brightest of miracles or the heaviest of woes.* Is it any wonder, therefore, to learn that the man's final vision was that of his heart aloft in the hand of the woman of his dreams, triumphant in her love?"

"You, my husband," I'd told Clarence, then, "are nothing less than a magnificent fiend."

"And you, my wife," Clarence said, "are a wonderful patron. You were as spellbound, it appears, as one who had looked upon the Hand of Glory itself."

"That may be so," I said, rubbing against him, "but it was no *hand* that ensorcelled this poor girl."

"No?" he said.

"*Trickster*," I said.

"Wench," he said.

"Casanova," I said.

"Lean back," he said, "and close your eyes."

"What will I see there?"

"Visions of sugar plums and fairy queens, methinks. Lean back."

"Transport me," I said.

"Your wish, madam, is my command."

"Now who," I said, "is being mawkish?"

"Forgive me, my lady."

"Never mind all that," I said. "Just do as you promised."

"Gladly," Clarence said, "gladly," and kissed me, there, and let go, there, with a deep hot breath that washed all through me like bliss from a spike. "Are your eyes closed?" he said when I shivered.

"*Tightly*," I said. "Please don't ever stop."

And I remembered also those cool spring nights spent bathing in wreathes of incense, and afternoons in autumn through the park, the lowing of klaxons by the sea, voices from the brush, children squabbling, parents calling, masters to dogs and lovers to beloveds, and, beneath it all, the cosmopolisian fugue.

Sundays in the sheets, them I thought of, too, torpors, endless, of promises and dreams, and lunches of potato chips, and dinners of red wine, and many a blood-spat sink, likewise, many a bit of green in the teeth while laughing in a crowd at an evening soiree.

The shades of mottled underwear haunted our days, the renegade clippings of nails in the sofa and boogers by the bed, the pubic-hair bathtubs and snot-filled rags.

We played peek-a-boo baby and dribbled honey on pears.

We talked on phones, we folded clothes, we cut our fingers and dusted blinds.

Our life, in other words, had no more been a litany of bliss than some olio of insects and waste on the sill.

It was simply—or so I'd thought, and think I did, for a long time indeed—a life spent chasing common interests—a happy marriage, as it were.

Until I pushed through the flames.

Ha!

All of it a vast simulacrum.

All of it a confusion of the thing with its idea, inexorably mounting toward my night of heaving dismay, lost, though just for a time, thank God, in a vertigo of doomed interpretation.

How fitting, then, that I should've been so ill in the moment of my enlightenment, that my physical state should have matched my mental. How fitting, yes, and how cathartic.

I didn't know it at the time, but those hours of revulsion in my cottage with Merle were the best thing that could have happened. Like a woman slowly poisoned, I was disgorging in an instant all those years of rust and fang.

I was dying, essentially, that I could live.

To think that to the moment Clarence died I'd thought myself as all but unwanted.

To believe he'd wrapped me in the wisdom of his days, given me to see the meaning of friendship, and of faith and trust and love, all the things I'd once thought shapeless and cold in a world where what had seemed to matter most was a nasty bottom line.

I was nineteen when we met in 1954, in the classical section of the record store, of course.

He had Chopin's *Nocturnes*. He had Wagner's

Götterdämmerung and *Die Walküre*. There was something by Pablo Casal, as well, *Bach's Suites for Cello*, I think.

In the music of the cello, he'd said more than once, *can be heard the weeping of the dark gods themselves. The cello is for me the portal to the very soul of dusk.*

When I told him how much I loved Bernard Herrmann's use of the cello in his scores, Clarence suggested that though he was disappointed by Mr. Herrmann's conspicuous absence from Hitchcock's latest film, *Rear Window*, he'd nevertheless be honored, if not delighted, were I to accompany him to see it.

I remember that evening better than most.

Leaving the theater topsy-turvy, panting in the drizzle, strange for September.

At Edy's for coffee and pie, the booth beside two men in turtlenecks and black berets.

Clarence had taken the glove from my hand, and then, caressing my fingers, slowly, lightly, one by one, gazing into my face with his sad blue eyes, he'd said, *You've got the heart of a peasant and the mind of a queen. Did you know you're more lovely than Grace Kelly could ever hope to be?*

My blushing had encouraged him, clearly.

You could tame beasts with your eyes, he said, *kings with your lips. If you'll let me, I'll kill spiders for you all day long.*

We were married three days later, and for seven years more, the two of us growing together, I'd thought, teaching one another, I'd thought, how to be and not to be.

And though clearly he was a man—fifteen years my senior, in fact—for all our hopelessly short-lived years I was still just a girl, really, I was still only learning what it meant to live in a world without fear.

We shot melons in the Capay Valley, shucked oysters at Tomales Bay. We ate olives beneath a sheet of tin and listened to the thrumming rain.

He was mine, I'd believed, for the rest of my days.

I hadn't even had to sprinkle those olives with chay-herb powder or mustard seed. It had never crossed my mind.

And why would it? I'd been content as a butterfly.

We were so happy that despite his prolonged trips, I never once felt an itching in my palms, never once felt a rend, however puny, in my supreme confidence, not just in *us*, Clarence and me, but in myself, as well, though now I know that it was every bit a little kiss from Judas.

Then one day I found him in the shower, cold as the stone the doctors said he'd dropped like when the heart attack hit him.

The paramedics handed me his ring and watch, then carted him away in a zippered bag.

Women were shopping across the way, busy with their flowers and meat. An old man had reclined on his porch to smoke his pipe and feed the birds. There was a toddler with a ray gun, killing his Talking Beanie Boy.

With a single blow, my rock of ages had become a clod of days, then it was washed away.

Once again I was the outcast I'd been.

Once again I'd been taken by the hand, as lightly as

had Clarence himself that long-ago night, and returned to the fogs of exile.

And there was no one to find me, and no one who wanted to find me.

Years went by, two or three at least, without my so much as glancing at a man. But that was my doing, and my choice. It wasn't that I hadn't wanted to look and didn't, but that I *couldn't*. I was too overwhelmed with, what, with the ghost of Clarence, I guess, with the void that had opened in his passing and left me to maunder dimensionless, like a soul in outer space.

But if his name alone was a spell, his belongings were a juggernaut.

I couldn't bring myself to discard them, either, yet neither could I bear to touch or see them—his tie, his comb, the nib of his pen—without lapsing into madness.

It got so bad at times I'd wake from a stupor smearing jam on the iron, or brewing a pot of Lysol tea, or even, one horribly shameful occasion, trying to stuff a clock in my vagina.

I called hardware stores, plumbers, lumberyards, clerks. And gardeners and roofers and mechanics, as well, I called these and more with the questions of fools—do you sell string? what types of leaks do you fix? can you plant seeds that grow into flowers? how long does it take for a car to run out of gas?—and I did it, mad as it seems, to hear the voice of a man, the heart behind his voice, the ache and the woe, though all along, I now know, I was hoping to hear but an echo of Clarence, heedless of the scorn in that voice, the incredulity, I admit, the alarm, and the pity, too.

There's no better way to a feeling of power, I soon learned, than to become an object of pity, because there's no better way to abjection. Which, if you think about it, is just another way of saying what's always been said: once you hit bottom, there's no place to go but up.

At last I found the means to leave the house, aware sometimes of the date, even of the hour and day of a sitcom like *Bewitched*. Still, hardly would I have departed than I'd know my effort pointless.

It had never been a matter of my not looking at men, but of men not looking at me.

Because the men were not looking at me—*ever*.

I judged this apathy, in the beginning, more as coolness than neglect, the natural response to a woman in grief. The men had seen my pain. I wore it like a suit of weeds. *She doesn't need some guy groping up her skirt, come on*, and etceteras.

After the hole I'd just crawled out of, what else could I believe?

But I may as well have been living in a can.

I'd invested in clothes, nitwit that I was, entire wardrobes of pencil skirts and blue jeans, mini-skirts even and too-bright tights, trouser suits of corduroy, Lurex, and tweed. I wore them double-breasted with Courtelle sweaters and tops of PVC. I threw away my winklepickers and went in for sling-backs with buckles and tongues. I painted my eyes with kohl, even, and my mouth with lipstick white as teeth.

I sat in cafés with my newly coiffured five-point reading books like *The Ginger Man*, while in my lap were the newest

LPs by the Dave Clark Five and Dusty Springfield, and those pretty-boy mop-heads from England.

My journal, of course, lay open for any who cared to see, filled with such quotes as, *If you're going to love somebody, love somebody who needs it*, all in my largest, most magisterial script.

I would hum Dione Warwick's "Walk on By" when entering a crowd of men, unable to suppress a grin, and this for having fancied myself, it was true, engaged in some vamped up Augustan wit.

At night, in bed, chasing my flimsy conquests, I'd remind myself that *every tulip is a julep and all the mint is meant for me*.

Hyperbole, I know, is the swiftest way between two points, and yet the power of litotes should never go unsung. Imagine, for instance, the desolation you'd feel in the refusal of your most violent craving. Then, to sweeten the pot, as they say, multiply that despair by, what, by eternity, say.

My days, I mean, had resolved into a torpor of pigs, of watching men lured to this girl and that without a wink in my direction.

I began to seek out the ugliest of women, split-lipped women, buck-toothed women, women with wall-eyes and piles.

I found them with tumors. I found them with boils. I found them with palsy and brash, jaundice and VD, wherever they were I found them out, crippled, clumsy, crude, the worse-off the better—amputees, for example, were the cream of the curdled crop.

Like a strumpet I loitered on streets with billboards for cigarettes and brandy, where yellow-eyed men in sharkskin suits passed me up for junkies with their spoons.

There were the midnight laundromats, the endless nameless sedimental bars.

And if these weren't enough, in addition to the charities, Salvation Armies and such, I found every halfway house I could, every rotten rehab I could, and name a fly-by-night place for fishes and loaves, and you were sure to spot me.

Nothing, in short, was too mean, and no one ever too low. There wasn't a place I couldn't be found if in the end it meant I might meet so little as a glance.

This went on, like some diabolical Mobiüs strip, until one Oakland night—one very hollow *West* Oakland night, I might add—a man in a bar walked right through me, the way ghosts are said to walk through walls.

Finally I understood.

This lack of interest in me, these unimpassioned men, their failure so much as to notice me: none of it had word one to do with them and the world to do with me, a flaw so persistently, glaringly evident that it must have become as inconspicuous to me as the scar on your face that day by day softens in the kindness of a mirror.

In the end, I was left with no choice but to assume that, one, I didn't exist, or, two, that I'd been cursed, perhaps for eternity, though at the least for life.

And then, dear God, my Era Vulgaris, then my weeks of middling fears and obsessive-compulsive rigmaroles, the dolor before kids with glassy eyes, afternoons with files and dust, nights at home pouring through all things history, reference, science—medicine, magick, superstition, astrology, numerology, tarot, shamanism, runes, witch craft, channeling, nightmares, koans, herbology, ascension, talismans, voodoo, Blavatsky's Lemuria and modern Wicca, and hypnotherapy and amulets and augurs of every sort, and prophets and messiahs of every sort, and that's to say nothing of the biographies, my Ouija board dabblings at the break of sunless dawns.

I learned what it meant to hold a skyclad ceremony, to receive the Fivefold Kiss of a Wiccan high priestess, one each for the feet, the knees, the penis, breasts, and lips.

I defined words like *esbat* and *athame* and committed to memory the eight sabbats of a year.

The magic prayers, yes, I learned them, also, the black and the white, a quest, I know, that could only have been for some meaning in the letters if not the words, the void around them even, however puny, but an inkling, dear God, of the reason for my thralldom and shame.

And the potions I played with, the countless manuals and countless guides—all for nothing, all for naught.

My longing was a sigh in the dark, a voice in a cellar while the storm raged on.

In my dreams I twined with kings, but when I came to, my bed was empty and the house cold.

It was museums, if truth be told, and books on art, that taught me finally the meaning of peace, in the paintings of suffering beyond compare, and the acts of resistance to powers that incur such awful fates.

Colombe's "Hell," for instance. Or *The Book of Hours* of Catherine of Cleves. Or two in particular by Blake—

"And Smote Job with Sore Boils," on the one hand, the magnificent "Satan, Sin, and Death" on the other.

Who was I to believe myself above the fray of life with its chances for calamity of body and soul?

Hell, St. John of Chrysostom tells us, *is paved with the skulls of priests.*

And when you look into a work of art that depicts such spoils, and you feel gripped by the claws of terror—that deep-in-your-heart, soul-cringing terror—you know, first, that the artist was great, lest otherwise you'd feel no more than mild annoyance for having wasted the time to look, and, second, that what you see there, the sublime horror, the intimation of some ever-shining blackness, is more likely than not but a hair's worth of pain come your day before the mighty Bar.

Humans, said Ellen Kay in her wisdom, *can no more promise to love or not to love than they can promise to live long. What they* can *promise is to take good care of their life* and *of their love.*

I had my snake, Tisiphone, I told myself, I had my children at school.

The years would show me the way.

Neither Jack nor The Ecdysiast had returned to the cottage that first night at Freedom Lake, caught up in their intrigues as they were.

Merle, it turns out, of all people, was my one sure thing.

In the typically gentle fashion I soon learned was his alone, he'd conveyed me to my door, then promised to return come morning, and did, my gang of obscene mishaps now in tow.

Each of them—Jomar, Jack, and the sweetly swooning Ecdysiast—as the scene eventually disclosed, had taken a massive dose of phenobarbital by way of dulling the biphetamine they'd spent the night gobbling down, courtesy of Wolfgang and Usch.

The sun was rising, though still the mountains hid it.

My room lay covered with that hazy pall of brass-colored light that with each day's coming makes the world seem everything's good, and yet I hadn't slept but for the haphazard snatch. And when actually I did grab a wink, it was to be assaulted by disfigured cherubs, their hair aflame, and defecating gressils, and jackals and crones, and endless piles of hacked-off limbs.

Tranquility, in short, had been a distant song.

I laid by turns atop the bed, sweating, scarcely able to breathe, or nested under blankets, my teeth a-rattle with chills.

I saw no relief.

I endured.

Then they arrived, laughing, Merle laughing at their laughing, which they hardly noticed, it seemed, or cared much if they did. It seemed, for that matter, they hardly noticed me, though how that could be I failed to gather, zombie that I was.

"Rachel-baby," Jack finally said, collapsing on the couch.

He'd forgotten how it was between us. It was his sweet-talking voice now, the voice that asked to rub his back.

"Roses are red," The Ecdysiast said, "and violets are blue, but guess what guys, my heart is really super purple, you know, like a giant purple crayon?"

"All those cats over in Nam right now," Jomar said, "losing this and that piece of flesh for a purple heart, and look, we're all swinging here groovy as berries and cream with so many purple hearts it's not even fair."

"I'm so purple," Jack said, "you could call me *blood*."

"*Purple*," The Ecdysiast murmured.

"Hallelujah for Wolfie and Usch," Jomar said. "That stuff of theirs has put me smack into the soul of the good Lord himself."

"Purple and pink and gold," The Ecdysiast said, "you know, Rachel?" Her eyes lazed about the room. "Have you ever felt, I don't know, just, you know, so purple?"

"*This*," Jack said, "is what you call like a rock and roller coaster."

And sure enough, with that, the three of them tumbled into laughter. It had them, now, all right, they were lost deep in it, stupidly beautiful in that maze, kingdom not of Bacchus but of his nitwit son.

"Look at you," Merle said, "wow, you really are burned, and I mean pretty severely, too. Maybe you should go to the doctor?"

He'd been holding out his hands as he spoke, just inches from my shoulders, wanting, I supposed, to comfort me with his touch, yet resisting the urge, knowing that this was the last thing I needed, however badly I'd wanted it, that it could only hurt me more than I'd already been.

I couldn't help myself, his eyes were too soft, his person too tender, and there it was, that belly of his—I poked it.

"I think you've got a leak."

And that was all it took to get us taken like the rest. Laughter had the bunch of us, now, we were all of us its witless slaves.

The room was filling with light, at last the sun had risen, and with it the aromatics of breakfast-in-the-works, bacon, eggs, biscuits, ham, the smoke from someone's fire, decorative only, I guessed, built perhaps in the spirit of this sylvan life, since already it was warm enough, as it were, to take off your clothes, and all of this mingled with the tang of redwoods and the trembling earth, the foraging moles, the leaves collapsing, the numberless flitting birds, and worms in the roots and moss on the stones, and birdsong, too, that was there, too, no less sweet in the passing than the moment itself, ambient, in any case, as the light on the walls, diffusely golden, goldenness divine, the whole of it so vital and deep that for a flash I'd nearly forgotten it could be as painful to laugh as cry.

Somewhere close the squealing of a girl dissolved into sobs, and then another shrieked.

And then a clutch of boys scampered by, and then, without so much as a titter, they were gone, and the girl's crying ceased, and still, unbelievably—how magnificent this life can be, how terrifically, awfully dreadful—we were laughing.

The world had returned.

Through the window, among the trees, people were moving, none of them in more than sneakers or thongs. At once strangely familiar and familiarly strange, these people were somehow distant, beings in a great cyclorama, and yet somehow, too, imminent, as near, it seemed, as Merle himself, whose breath like tangerines and syrup I could smell, whose hand hung so close to my thigh I could feel its heat. Some lingered talking. Others wandered on. And over each of their faces, as if maybe they'd left the same movie or yogi or trepanation center even, lay the expression not so much of bliss but, what, maybe just old-time contentment.

Doubtless this was more than a world of serenely humming robots.

Yet still it was difficult at first glance to tell each person from the next.

Their nakedness and their bemused expressions had lent them something like the sheen of uniformity. If you squinted, let your eyes go blurry, these people might've been doohickeys with penciled mouths and eyes.

And yet you only had to focus to see they were unique, to see them brimming with uniqueness even—beauty marks and birth marks, freckles, cleft palettes, hearing aids, lips as full as a swelling moon. Once you started, in fact, looking that is, they became so crazy with peculiarity that you could write a book—the different kinds of blue in a person's eyes, the varied shapes of human digits, the diversity of teeth, the hue of skin, the ten million textures of hair.

"By Ned!" Merle exclaimed. "I knew there was something I wanted to tell you all yesterday, but I guess I just kind of forgot about it, what with my being the big old dummy I am. It's Donald Duck," he said. "Yesterday was his *birth*day."

Jomar heard this and sat up to dig at his eye. Incorrigible he was, and would remain. He was giggling some, still, but even so, in a gurgling sort of way, he glided once more to the voice of that phony dad.

"I reckon I dropped quite a few beauties last night, there at the shank of a quite memorable evening, but you, my groovy panther of a cat, y'all must've slurped down a whole baggie of those gals. Donald Duck, man? You've got to be jiving me."

"What's so funny about Donald Duck?" I said. "Other than that he's funny?"

"I'd really love to meet him?" The Ecdysiast said. "He sounds fan*tas*tic."

"Now you're *all* trying to jive me," Jomar said.

"Honest," Merle said, holding up two banded fingers. "No biggie, though, it's just another one of those useless pieces of information people get stuck with now and then, kind of a parasitical factoid, if that makes any sense."

"Well, if he's useless," The Ecdysiast said, "then forget it?"

Jack's head was waggling and bobbing. "I'm on the verge," he said, still laughing, "of going to see if those dudes up in management have something we can pump her stomach out with. This is getting pretty freaky-deaky."

"Don't tell me he's a Textile or something," The Ecdysiast said. "Merle?"

"If you folks can maybe just donate a smidgeon of disbelief," Merle said, "and maybe, too, even pardon the expression as it were, I mean since he's just a cartoon character and what all, but it's as true as blue that the storks brought Donald Duck to the silver screen thirty-nine years ago to the day, to yesterday I mean, right, in 1934, that is, I'm pretty sure."

"Then you *are* for real," Jomar said.

"He just said it was Donald Duck's birthday," I said. "What's wrong with you people?"

"Don't even tell me you're calling a swim through the bossest purple haze ever *wrong*," Jack said.

"Purple haze—all through my brain!" Jomar shouted. "Lately things just don't seem the—"

"People," I said with my hands on my ears.

"You guys saw that burn of hers," Merle said, "and you know how you can get one of those tearing headaches when that happens, too, and the creepy-creeps and tummy-burbles sometimes even, which by the looks of it is what happened to Rachel here if I can see a cloud in the sky and so forth and such."

"Rachel?" The Ecdysiast said, and lurched away from the now-sleepily-mumbling Jack to stroke my head. "I'm so sorry?"

"Jenny-baby," mumbled Jack. That was it. He had had it, the man was down for the count.

"We're all just a little torqued, I guess," Jomar said, spiking his voice faintly with remorse. "But dig, Rachel, you don't have to worry any, because no matter what, you're still right up there at the top of the heavy fantastics."

It was then that things grew whooshy again.

My vision went dim at the edges, I was nauseated, too, and when finally my head had cleared enough to make out this from that, Jomar was in the midst of, what, a *rant*.

"... I mean for *real*," he was saying. "I mean as in *really* real, as in a no-matter-what kind of real, you know? Like so really real it'd be like trying to drag the foxy out of you, and that, man, would be about as crazy as trying to drag the good out of my man JC, you dig what I'm saying, baby, so really real that . . ."

And still The Ecdysiast was stroking my head. "Your hair is *so* beautiful," she said. "I only hope by the time I'm your age maybe I can be so lucky?"

"Rachel really could use a rest, probably," Merle said. "Not that I'm trying to be rude or anything guys, I completely respect where you're coming from, and actually I even know just what you mean, about your colors and so forth. *But.*"

"What *you* need," The Ecdysiast said, "is maybe an amethyst on your brow, Rachel, at the sixth chakra I think, to, you know, open up your third eye?"

91

"Donald Duck," Jomar said.

He'd been talking all this while, surprisingly so, gibbering honestly, which was the last thing I'd expect from the man, mostly about how *foxy* I was, and how *heavy*, and how hard it would be to make me other, and when now and then he did digress one way or the next it was to return to the subject of my *totally mind-blowing foxiness*.

"But that is one funky cat, I'll agree, dig?" he said, headed back for unknown reasons to good old Donald Duck. "And that's cool, too, man, he's pretty funky for an old jive-ass cat like that you know, duck, I mean, what with his going around without any pants and that, but what I'm talking about, man, is like those other little dudes that're always hanging around and getting him all far out away from Safetytown or Schmuckburg or wherever it is they hang, Pooey and Dewey and those little squirts, you know? And that old cluck Spooge or whoever—"

"*Jo Jo*," The Ecdysiast said, "didn't you hear what Jacky told us about that Duck guy being real scary and maybe even a Textile? There's so much more to life than clothes. Gosh, I thought you were hip to that already?"

"You want to know what I'm hip to?" said the apostate. Boy, was he really stooping. Here he was, pulling one I'd scarcely have expected from Jack. "*Ughhh!*" he said, with a thrust of his pelvis. "You don't watch out, I'm going to sock it to you, baby!"

"Not with any Textile around you won't."

"It's true, Jenny, I'm not a duck, okay? I mean, dig, it's true I'm not even like a swan. But what's guaranteed *not* true is I don't know a thing or two about a thing or two."

"Probably," Merle said, "and seriously, this isn't a joke, but it's pretty possible that Jenny's the type of woman who needs to see a thing with her own eyes before she'll believe it. Probably."

Jomar caught The Ecdysiast by her hand. "Are you with it, baby? Are you ready to, you know, do the lo-co-*mo*-tion?"

I couldn't believe it, though neither did I care very much by then, but The Ecdysiast actually blushed.

"*Jo Jo*," she said.

"Jo Jo nothing," the apostate said, and started for the door.

"But what about my shades?"

"You don't need them where we're going," Jomar said, and winked at Merle. "Come on, Sexy, we'll just take a little dip in the pool."

"There you go," Merle said, "great idea, very nifty."

"And then after that, we'll take a dip in the *pool*, if you know what I mean, and I think you do know what I mean."

The Ecdysiast looked like a woman who'd just got off a bus in a foreign town. "You think you're funny, Jo Jo, but you're not."

Jomar did a two-step shimmy while bobbing his head like young James Brown.

"Funny, sunny, runny," he said. "Call me anything you like, Hot Pants, just so long as it's not late for that sweet chicken dinner I *know* you got going on!"

He'd taken her hand again. Already they were out the door, stumbling through the sun.

"Yes!" Jomar shouted. "Good *God* almighty—yes!"

Merle sat beside me, on the sofa's arm. I could smell him, his musky cleanness, his freshly shampooed head.

"What I told you about Donald Duck's birthday?"

"It's okay," I said, sensing an apology. "Really."

"See, it's more like I only know about all that, what I said about his birthday and so forth, because, well, because that's *my* birthday, too, kind of stupid, I know, but true, more than a raindrop actually, no kidding."

That Merle would've said that, then, at that moment, was as fitting as could be. In the flesh, shod but naked, nervously grinning and yawning—a lovely black man, he was, a funny white duck.

For the first time, our hands met and stayed.

"Just who are you, anyway?"

"My uncle saw him in his first feature the day I was born, Donald Duck, I mean, in a movie theater in LA, I guess. He was smoking a cigar that even had my name on it. In the end, he told me, the wise little hen fed Donald Duck and Peter Pig castor oil. Read into that, why don't you," Merle said, and let go my hand to pat his belly, "you know, the symbolism and everything like that, and everything else, wow. It's a wonder my name isn't Donny." He was massaging his belly now, shaking his head, too. His eyes had grown curiously shifty. "As a matter of fact, it's a wonder I haven't fallen over with hunger already. I'm so hungry, Rachel, I could cuss."

"Maybe you'd like a bowl of hotdog soup?"

"Steal my teeth, is that what you're trying to do?"

"Not before you eat," I said.

"So then you *do* want to head to the Wagon. Let me

tell you, they serve up one heck of a meal, heavy or light, depending on your fancy, sprouts and carrots and yogurt and all if you care for that sort of thing, or perchance you're the kind of gal who watches her figure, which to me it looks like you are, and then sure all that other good old stuff, French toast and so forth that's pretty excellent if you ask me."

"What I need," I said, "is rest."

I threw Jack's legs off the sofa, to lie down, but he bolted up scowling.

"I hope for your sake there's a fire," he snarled, "because that shit there is certifiably bogus."

"Go back to sleep. Go get in bed."

"Hold on a sec," Jack said, his eyes darting. "Where's Jenny?"

"Hunger, Jack, is a most mighty thing," Merle said. "For instance, did you know a man is more likely to commit a violent crime when he's hungry than when he's not? They say it's heat sets them all off, but you can bet your granny the pernicious little penguin behind most of this nastiness we've got going on and so forth, and this is only generally speaking, is good old Mister Hunger Pang himself."

Jack had been picking at a scab on his knee. Now that Merle had finished, he flipped a piece of it onto the rug.

"So then where is she, Rachel?" he said. "I mean *them*, where are they?"

"Who?"

"Jenny and that Jomar dude, man, *come on.*"

I turned to Merle. "Hadn't Jomar said something about them taking a dip in the pool, and then, what, taking a dip in the *pool*?"

"More or less you could say those were his exact words I think."

Over his shoulder, on a brass-buckled strap, Jack carried a leather satchel embossed with painted flowers and vines. It contained the grass I bought him—what else—and all his *amigos chibos*, this expression, I figured, his attempt at some kind of cool ethno-shibboleth he'd recently adopted for his drug paraphernalia, lifted, no doubt, from the beatnik-cum-hippies with whom he was wont to laze away his time. In his stupor, the man must've forgotten he had the thing, because, as if taken by a panic, he began to slap at where his pockets would've been while muttering about *a toke of spleef.*

Merle touched the weirdo's knee.

"Alls you have to do is look at that gruesome burn Rachel's got to see she's not going to be sweating her way through a ping-pong match or anything like that, and that's just about forgetting your regular old day-to-day thises-and-thats. But you, Jack, given you're game and all, how'd you like to join me over at the Wagon for a little top-of-the-morning-type munchathon?"

Jack stood up. He diddled with his ponytail and picked at his ear and stamped his big-toed feet.

"I forgot something," he said.

"Whatever it is," I told him, "it can wait. Go on now, Jack, go to sleep."

"But it's my license," he said, ridiculously. "I think I lost my license."

And that was it—before we could speak, the man was rushing down the path, his monstrosity aswing.

Truly he was vexed—ha—and I knew why. Jomar

Links was as familiar with the notion of *carpe diem* as he was with a good thing. She'd played smack into his hands, The Ecdysiast had, and while she was at it, right out of Jack's. I imagined the vertigo that must've been swelling inside him, like rice in a bird.

Jack didn't have a license, and had never had, not even one to fish.

Through the screen, Merle said, "Don't forget what I said about that hunger, Jack. Go to the Wagon. They've got real superlative fare."

"I'm sorry," I said.

"You'll pardon me, Rachel, but that's totally unacceptable. It's *me* who should be apologizing, the boinker-head I am that keeps forgetting how burned you are and sick and everything. I'm sorry for not thinking of *you*. Wow."

"And yet here you are anyway, right?"

"I'll tell you what. Hows about I run up to the Wagon for a quick bite while you hop into the old hay again? By the time you wake up, I'll have something ready for you to nibble on."

And now the sun was very high.

No longer purple and pink and gold, but only gold, and flaming blue, the sky was shimmering, and the trees were shimmering, I heard that sweetly frightful horn again, somewhere across the camp, and the flip and flop of sandals, a calisthenics man barking drills above a song— *all summer long grooving in the sand, playing Sgt. Pepper's Lonely Hearts Club Band*—and so I closed my eyes, I opened and closed my eyes, happily sadly dizzy.

A breeze through the window set the curtains swimming.

Sleep. It was there to be had. I heard the call of bed.

"Sure, *Donny*," I said. "Whatever you want."

"Sure?"

With two fingers, I jiggled Merle's pinky.

"Quack, quack," I said.

The man was beaming as he left.

"And Donny," I said. "Happy *birth*day."

Merle had drawn a bath and brought me flowers, too, sweetly—if crudely—assembled, gathered from the meadow.

In less than a day we'd cut through a lifetime of diffidence and error. The useless formalities, the vital umbrage, all this and more we'd promptly shed for an intimacy that, while odd, was easily enough sustained.

I languished through the day with him, this new naked man, who for reasons inexplicable had assumed the role of patient mate.

I listened to the water as he draped his finger through the suds, and the melody of leaves and birds, the seemingly animate cottage lightly creaking or groaning in the breeze.

I held his hand, I looked into his eyes.

He began to stammer, but the words fell short.

I said nothing. I simply held his hand.

And he held mine, and we remained for a long, quiet while.

Despite the nausea that erupted with each foray to my past, I made up my mind to learn what Merle could tell me about the other side of the illusion that had been my life for seven years.

In the days that passed before I could leave the cottage, Merle shared what he'd known before I'd arrived, and all he discovered since.

Wolfgang and Usch, as it happened, weren't the only folks at Freedom Lake who'd been privy to my husband's feats. Merle himself had met him on numerous occasions, as had nearly all the locals come the end of August.

My dear departed demon, it appears, had been a regular.

This, however, wasn't to say he'd been merely a common swinger. Among other things, or rather primarily, the evidence revealed that Clarence was a prankster, and even, really, what most today would call a crook.

In this capacity he was the leader of a band of Situationist-like topplers known as The Ministry of Obvious Discontent.

His purpose in life—it had not, appalling though it was to confess, centered round his ever-loving wife— had been to subvert all such notions as work, play, and media as we know them, all organization, all hierarchy, even, if wonders can be believed. As far as Clarence was concerned, I was told, the political left was actually the right and the right was just plain wrong, and he wanted nothing to do with either.

Instead, as the Ministry's alleged director, Clarence spent his days struggling to achieve *truly* spontaneous self-expression, *truly* unhampered inspiration, *truly* open-minded sex.

With varying levels of censure and praise, depending on whom you asked, of course, it was said among the circles in which Clarence used to run that he couldn't be satisfied with anything less than the total exaltation of imagination and desire. Moreover, though—and somehow this brings a kind of twisted pleasure to what might otherwise have been a load of hurt—my husband had achieved his ends beneath the seemingly innocuous guise of Mr. Everyday himself, a sort of Joe Conformity, as it were.

But the difference between my definition of tricky and his left oodles to be preferred. I was as dumb to my husband's ways, in the scope, by God, as the dead to the dirt they're in.

Notwithstanding this gulf, however, when finally Merle told me how Clarence had managed, in his way, to pollute the mainstream of attitudes with his notions, even as he rowed through its midst, well, it was enough to bloat me with pride.

What can you say about a man who, after taking the guise of a doctor, had not only slipped into a prison to test the effects of LSD on its individuals, but also, for three straight years, to take the drugs himself, *in* the prison, with the *prisoners*—murderers and rapists and molesters and such—and then, for a real *mind blow*, for an honest-to-goodness *fait accompli*, in the end to get the pardon of these rascals, none of whom, as the tale is told, were recidivists?

What can you say about a man who'd invented a *language of the ineffable* for a propaedeutic literature endorsed by the Mayor of San Francisco and its Chamber of Commerce, literature, moreover, that was posted as handbills in suburban tracks and country malls, all with titles such as "You Too Can Kill Your Boss," "Stealing as a Healthy Way of Life," and "There Is Life Before Death"?

Yes, and what can you say about a man who'd exhibited in the freezers of industrial slaughterhouses pictures of lactating women bound and gagged?

Who along the blind turns of highways outside middling towns had fashioned barricades of stones and trees and reported accidents in the night for no reason more than to watch the Powers That Be smash against them?

Who'd sent marijuana by mail as gifts to strangers whose names he'd got from phone books?

Who'd conducted retreats whose goal was to achieve the state of self-sufficiency he called *autarkeia*, got by journeys on hands-and-knees through tunnels at whose ends, the participants were assured, they'd meet the wisest man alive, but instead, under the influence of LSD, found themselves staring into mirrors?

Who at night had burned into country-club golf greens slogans such as GOD HAS A HARD-ON FOR REPUBLICANS and GUNS ARE GOOD BUT BOMBS ARE BETTER!?

Who long before Alan Abel came along had dressed horses and cows and pigs in bathing suits and Bermuda shorts, evening gowns and muumuus, all in protest of their nakedness?

Who'd used subsonic sound to terrorize neighborhood bullies into wholesale flight?

Who'd planted commodities on supermarket shelves, cereal and soup and cakes, each with photos on the front of roadkill, fungus, crash victims, freaks?

Who after commandeering city buses had driven the passengers, most of them unaware they'd left their routine, to various hinterland destinations, waste management sites, for example, or sewage treatment plants, where as he abandoned them explained that the *tour* was from that point on *self-guided*?

Who in the guise of an exterminator had entered gymnasiums, businesses, courthouses, homes, public schools, and DMVs—among others—not to rid them of vermin but to infest them with the multitudes in his grip?

Who in fancy restaurants and corporate lobbies had conversed with masturbating men and women, and not beneath the tablecloth, mind, or behind the flowerpot strategically placed, but openly, for all to see with disbelieving eyes?

Who'd delivered to gala events giant cakes full of Cheese Wiz, and then, at various moments of truth, the upper crust gathered about these treats in ritualistic expectation, had plastered them head to toe by exploding the bombs in the glop?

Who'd poured butyric acid into the night deposit boxes of every bank in a given town?

Who'd killed spiders for his lover all day long?

What, really, *can* you say?

Insofar as I could gather, Clarence had founded his bureau in the mid-'50s, just around the time we met.

His activities, to quote Merle, himself quoting someone else, constituted *a surrealist-inspired attack on the clockwork of alienated consumption and the swinish values of the endlessly zombified Babbitry.*

And it was because of Clarence, moreover, his underground stature, the foundation he'd lain, that people like Paul Krassner could start *The Realist*, that Krassner could play such rumors as the one in which Lyndon B. Johnson was said to've fornicated with the wound in JFK's throat as he lay in state in Air Force One—*functional necrophilia*, Krassner had called it—a desecration whose motive (if Jackie's word to Gore Vidal held any truth, that she'd seen the President laughing above her husband's casket) could only have been to enlarge the size of the hole in her husband's throat to make the Warren Commission believe Lee Harvey Oswald had been the single killer!

It was because of Clarence, said the regulars at Camp Freedom Lake, that the Situationists of today, *those quasi-radicals*, as with obvious disdain they were called by some, in that, I suppose, they really were too visible—groups like Point-Blank!, Diversion, Contradiction, and those— well, folks claimed it was because of Clarence that these bodies could exist at all, that someone had thought even to create them.

It's also worth mentioning that this Ministry of Obvious Discontent was never what Clarence himself had called it. Nor had he so much as thought of it as a *group*, much less a group that was "his." For him, there was no such thing to have belonged to. And without a group to lead, it follows, Clarence could never have been its leader.

For Clarence, to have created something to name and belong to would've been to commit the grossest of hypocrisies.

The moment we make a body we can name, one man or many, he'd said, that body is done. Made, it's nameable, but power, Clarence held, real power—the skill to make people do what they never had or would—rose from secrecy, from the freedom, as it were, from liability.

And that this law, if so we can call it, was the source of my husband's strength, was evinced by me myself.

Not one chirp, in other words, had I heard about his doings, nor had I suspected the least.

They'd been as present as gravity, and as unseen.

The list of people gone mad in the wake of a catastrophe that shatters their vision of the world is as long as it is well-documented, but we need only witness Ophelia's response to Hamlet's psychosis to see why I had to learn who Clarence was.

Next to my husband's hoax on me, a crime in every way, Hamlet and his were from Sunday morning comics.

The Real, I came to see, had terrified Clarence as much as it had charmed him. Like a rattle on a nursery floor, The Real had been for Clarence nothing short of magic. And while its sounds had never ceased to make him laugh, the source of those sounds, the machine at their core, had kept him just the same tethered to the stake he'd driven into darkness.

The wise man's greatest terror lies in the chance he no longer be afraid. This is why, as Baudelaire has noted, *he never laughs but that he trembles.*

No wonder The Real had been to my husband master and servant both. It must have been for him, I thought, a stroll through a nightmare to gorgeous to escape.

Ah, to be taught by the ghost of a phantom.

To laugh at terror in the midst of terror.

To play it to an end that never comes.

How, for mercy's sake, could my presence at this camp not have been for anything but naught?

No more thumbing my nose at the little things. No more dancing in a dark that was only ever my shadow.

Coincidence, I saw, is a buffoon made by us from an order we can't fathom. Afraid to say what we don't know, we smear the things beyond us as chaos in the void. But now I was better. Now I knew what I'd not known had been for my own good, I cozied up to my buffoons and let them entertain me.

Beats me, sure, but the next thing you know I'd become a celebrity, if that's the right word, or perhaps *curiosity* is more like it, though that's not right, either, especially when the notion is further in-between, since, after all, when you think about it, what are celebrities if not *curiosities*, people whom everyone knows but rarely understands, endowed, somehow, if only consensually—which is to say superficially—with a peculiar luminescence that's as obvious as mysterious and draws the world to them like blood draws sharks, and this can be the case whether they're an actor or a dog—witness Rin Tin Tin or Ronald Reagan, the governor, for crying out loud!—so much so, obviously, that others are driven both to inquire about these people and to covet them, study them, stalk them, even to pattern cults around them, all without knowing any more about the human they've glorified than the pixels that make their image on a screen or in the paper or magazine, though sometimes it's less than that, sometimes it's just a voice they've heard, on the radio of a bus perhaps or from a neighbor's car being polished in the weekend shade, though sometimes, too, less than that, much less than that will suffice, a snippet of talk, for example, the weest of wee white lies, one here, one there, a name on paper, blobs of ink, fact and fiction mounting till a person's smallest, most commonplace histories and routines have attained the gravest import, from their hometown swimming holes and mothers' maiden names to the way they wipe their bottoms and the brands they use to do it, it's so awfully sad, if only someone told them all how silly or resplendent, since it must be one if not the other, I don't know, maybe it was I who was confused, yes, *it's better to be wise than rich*, as it's said, I really do know, I do.

But whatever the case, no one knew me, not Merle and certainly not Jack, nor had I committed some noteworthy feat.

And yet for all of that, or for none of it, in a ridiculous day and a half I'd somehow become "famous" at Freedom Lake. I say *somehow* only because it seemed impossible that Merle's spreading my name about had been enough to have bestowed on me this appalling status. Wolfgang and Usch had helped him, no doubt, but still.

Late Monday morning I woke to a roomful of flowers, store-bought and wild, and gifts, as well, abundant gifts, intriguing gifts, the gifts of strangeness from strangers.

One woman gave me a towel she'd spent the night embroidering with my name, a *courtesy cloth*, Merle called it, for laying across public furniture, poolside, for instance, or at the picnic tables round the Wagon.

There was a cribbage board with ivory pegs shaped after the silhouettes of women, its deck of cards backed by naked people, men and women plus children, too, singly and together, a special edition hot from the presses of the INF.

Another kind lady, Merle said, having heard me complain of thirst the day I'd arrived, brought me a thermos imprinted with cute little mice in bonnets and shawls, filled with pineapple juice, no less.

Yet another gave me a boiled egg painted with the words, WE LOVE YOU, RACHEL!

There was a sheaf of knitting needles, a bottle of Charlie perfume, three pulp fiction novels, an oil painting, crude as can be, of Rodin's *The Kiss*, a bar of soap on a rope—from some brute, I imagined—a package of Black Jack chewing gum—from the same brute's son, I'm sure—an oil-paper parasol dappled with cherry blossoms and scalloped, to boot, a jar of mud called Down to Earth, which, surprisingly enough, I'd seen on television shows such as *To Tell the Truth* and *What's My Line?*

There were magazines, too, *Helios, Sun Era, Nudism Today*, a remedial book for those who can't help themselves, entitled—ha—*Understanding Fear in Ourselves and Others*.

Just what did I have that others did not, *moi*?

People, after all, came to wish me well, even, in a way, to pay me homage. They flooded me with gifts as surely as you glut a beast or shrine.

When I asked Merle what it was all about, how this phenomenon could've come to pass, he answered, simply, "They like your hair."

They liked my hair!

Well, of course they did—what else? And where would I've been without it, this ever-so-precious hair?

For weeks before we left Jack had stressed the pettiness of *appearance* among the good folk of Freedom

111

Lake. I'd rather slither down the street with a rash on my face, I'd told him, than leave without my do. Lounging naked in the woods with a pack of naked pervs, I'd told him, that idea was revolting as the smell of boiling eggs. *Creepy,* I'd said in grotesque frisson, as if my impending nudity were a hole of worms into which I was being made to stick a hand.

And that my hair now had a thing to do with this weird reception made nausea seem like love.

What would these strangers think were I to lose my hair, were my hair to be burned, for instance, or, less, to be shaved away, as Jack had once scornfully suggested, such that I was as *bald as a baby rabbit*?

Would they be wrenching their necks with gawking then? Would they make themselves pilgrims then, bearing their strange little gifts? Quite obviously I was no Jean Harlow, no Grace Kelly or Veronica Lake. They were all so far away from me, these divas, distant as a star from Earth.

What had I been thinking that day at Earl's Odyssey of Hair?

What was it I'd hoped to achieve through such a measly transformation, this assumption into the Realms of Blonde?

How could this abundance of golden hair possibly hide the blatancy I was, the aging diffident schoolmarm I was, unlovable and unloved?

Had I really believed it could do the same for others, much less transfix them into ogling worship?

It was all quite past me, quite. And that I'd been thrust into this situation—requiring my public nudity, and for the first time ever, mind, since the day I'd been set to gibber among this peanut gallery of souls—did nothing but radically complicate my world.

There I was, naked, and blonde, now, too, exposed to this horde of strangers. How was I to radiate charisma, confidence, aplomb, much less boo about tranquility?

A life spent believing myself the stepchild of red, and suddenly I was to do all of *this*?

But isn't this what I'd wanted, to be wanted, to be pursued like a precious stone, to know a clamor would trace my every step—*What is it, that perfume she's wearing, it must be Yardley's* Oh de London, *but so then you've heard she's an actual contessa, widowed and—No, no, no, a baroness exiled and in disguise is what Erma said, did not, did so, did not did so did not*?

Or was this only what I'd *thought*?

The situation, alas, had grown more complex than my having become what they thought. To begin, there was Jack to consider, to say nothing of, what, the unexpected *unions* between myself and Merle, and Jomar and The Ecdysiast.

Somehow Jack had managed to thrust himself into the terribly goofy center of things, or, more accurately, to've got placed as such by forces past his say. This was understandable. Between our arrival and my recovery—when at last my burn had eased into a sheen of honeyed allure, and I'd regained a semblance of calm—so many developments had emerged that Jack of all people lacked the means to withstand their power.

It was clear, to me and the rest, that once The Ecdysiast had been lost in the sway of Jomar Links, not only was she helpless to escape, but in consequence Jack had been all but purged from her thoughts.

And no sooner had he seen the state of things, that now she was Jomar's slave—as indeed nothing could be less obvious, their little *affaire d'amour* was as clear as a sheet of polished glass, yes, the two were clearly heavily in lust and maybe even love—well, no sooner had Jack realized this than he'd slipped into the madness of a cuckold.

You'd think she'd have been resentful of his efforts to regain her favor, but no. The Ecdysiast went on as ever, in blithe vacuity, as though Jack were a stretch of sweltering days she'd resigned to bear.

More surprising still, her imperviousness to his antics did nothing to quell his fervor. With each new repulsion of his clownish salvos, he grew that much more pathetic. As the days grew hotter, so to speak, The Ecdysiast went increasingly for dips in the spring that ran among the trees and stones—over yonder, as they say—just across the boiling glade. All things good and bad, even she well knew, must perish in the end.

In short, The Ecdysiast had resolved to wait for Jack to tire and leave.

Dusk had fallen, late dusk, and we were at the pergola with its flowers and vines, The Ecdysiast and me and Merle, marveling with our vodka tonics at the power of the ecstasy all around.

It was the first since Saturday I'd stayed out for any time—four whole days vanished in a dream—and this on the advice of Merle, in consideration, he said, of the evening's coming fête. The freshness of the moment may have been the reason, or perhaps the onset of spirits in my head, but I was giddy with sensations, bright to the world, this and that impression, this and that idea, I couldn't help myself a bit.

Soften your eyes, I thought, and so I did.

The air hung fragrant with people, trees, drink, and smoke, a calliope of voice and song there was, laughter mostly but shrieking, too, the shrieking of joy, of youngsters through the forest, beneath the tables and in the pool, and birdsong and birdchatter, and the skrees overhead of a hawk. Moths had begun to bounce from the fields, and with them midges and mosquitoes, and there were bats in the sky, and swallows, as well, out past the blooming vines, dashing, twirling, diving.

The Ecdysiast saw the birds and, in her wild giggling way, said, "It's so *true*! And you don't even have to really trip on it to see it, what they're doing, you know, the birds?"

"No," I said. "You don't at all. They're *flying*."

It was as if I'd just told The Ecdysiast I was a bug. "But what does that *mean*," she said, "you know, to fly, artistically speaking I mean?"

"Maybe," Merle said, "if you'll allow me, that is, I can try to take a little bit of a stab at it."

"But can't you see? Gosh. It's so, I don't know, so *obvious*?"

Not for a trice did Merle's smile waver. "Naturally we don't want you to get, how's it go, your panties in a steam, analogically speaking of course, seeing as how, heh, you don't have a pair to speak of—surprise!—but I'll do the best I can, okay? *If*, of course, like I said, you don't mind."

"You're *so* cute," The Ecdysiast said.

"So, sure they're *flying*," Merle said, nodding toward the birds, "and pretty gorgeously, too, at least it looks pretty darn incredible to me, birds have always held a special place in this guy's ticker, yeah, I mean I've pretty often figured that's what I'd want to be if I had it to do again, a bird, maybe even one of those little guys right out there, they're so lovely and graceful—oops, sorry, believe it or not I *am* getting to where I'm going with this thing, Jenny—but so anyway, that's probably why you'd have thought what you just thought, at least that's what I figure, right, maybe? But then again, maybe I'm wrong and what *I'm* thinking has nothing to do with what *you're* thinking, or I guess maybe I should say what you *were* thinking, though we don't have to go there now either because if I *am* right, and pretty obviously that doesn't happen all too often, plus remember I'm just taking a stab at this, well, if I'm anywhere close to right, then I guess I'd have to say you were thinking of *dancing*, the birds I mean, that what they're really doing is *dancing*, I mean at least I hope so, wow."

The Ecdysiast was actually squirming.

You'd have thought her some vapid angel, a giddy vapid angel to Jomar's lusty cherub, the two of them so radiant and brazen they might well have been shining with the light of their own suns. But Jomar wasn't with us then—he'd gone to town on an errand—and still her face was a nexus of light.

Her teeth seemed animated, her fingers lithe as snakes. She had the toes of Salome, this woman, the tummy of a kid, warmly inviting, soft and smooth, there was a purity there, I suppose, and up and down her laughter was infectious. Of the ineluctable, this was the pull she had, despite that nothing about her, body or behavior, smacked the least of *effort*, of the smallest end of *thought*, and that, I imagine, was what set her apart, what made her the power she essentially was—a child, innocent and gay, attired in glamour, the elegance of a queen.

Listening to Merle, we'd lapsed into near-fixation. Whether he'd made his point or merely paused for breath we couldn't tell. Then The Ecdysiast saw with a rush of glee that he'd actually had his say, and she began to clap.

"Yes, Merle!" she said, and rose from her chaise to execute a pirouette. "You're *so* right *on*. Which, you know, if like flying birds are dancing, I mean, you could practically say that dancing people are *flying*, which is totally the way I feel whenever I'm doing it, dancing, I mean, on the stage, you know, or even right here, on this grass, beneath these flowers and this sky filled with all these gorgeous birds, you know, and all these beautiful people around me, too, it's so fan*tas*tic?"

Merle's eyes were bright, his smile brighter yet. "Sure," he said. "Definitely. Boy is that a good thing to hear. I'll bet you plenty I sleep well tonight!"

When Merle asked for my thoughts, it was hard to tell. Honestly, I told him, I couldn't pinpoint what he meant any more than I could say why The Ecdysiast was so worked up, however lovely the idea, that if a bird was flying it was dancing and that, likewise, people who are dancing are flying, though if nothing else I sensed it, what she was getting at. I hadn't danced for years, and certainly I'd never *flown*.

"Are you kidding?" Merle said, nigh on shouting. "Look at her, Jenny, would you, and tell me if you don't see right there before you a woman on fire with dance and flight?"

"Gosh, Rachel, that's half the reason I even thought of it, how beautiful you look tonight, because of your radiant skin and even like your soul and everything? It's like it's been released or something, I mean, like you're dancing and flying at the same time and all you have to do is just *sit* there!"

"You're too much," I said. "And even if you weren't, I'd

still have a hard time guessing what I've done to deserve your rolling out the red carpet this way."

"There are *lots* of people, Rachel, who've tried to do all sorts of stuff and never got anywhere, probably because of all the stuff they've done before, you know, it keeps getting in their way? And then there are people who haven't done *any*thing, what looks like anything to anyone else, I mean, and you'd think they were just filled with, I don't know, with diamonds and silver and gold? It's pretty incredible when you see it." I was slack-jawed with amazement. "Gosh, Rachel, when was the last time you looked in the mirror?"

"She did that, Jenny," Merle said, "she might go blind! She's so full of sunshine right now, next to her we could nab a tan at midnight."

"One thing's for sure," I said, taking her hand. "I've got nothing on you."

The Ecdysiast gathered up her breasts and pushed them my way. On her face was the beam of a Karma Sutra girl.

"You're so sweet, Rachel? But really, that's not what Jo Jo says, about what *you've* got, I mean? He saw you just before he left and said, *Like would you dig on that, Jenny? That lady there has got a secret if I've ever seen one. Man, I'd hate to be by myself when you and her went out on the town. You'd knock me dead, man—wham-bam-thank-you-mam!*"

"But you're actually beautiful," I said. "Me, I'm just nice, and that's on a good day."

"Do you think so?" Merle said. "I could be completely wrong, because that's the way it usually is, but maybe it'd be more accurate to say your *source*, to use an expression if that's okay with you, is just a little deeper."

I held Merle's eye. "Are you trying to tell me," I said, "I shouldn't be jealous?"

"What?" The Ecdysiast said, all at once consternated.

"Let me put it this way," Merle said. "Once, there was this bird, see. Now this was a special bird, a very beautiful bird, for all sorts of reasons, but mostly because it had *two heads*, right? Well, what happened was there came a day when one of the heads found a piece of most excellent manna, sorry, I know manna is excellent already or it wouldn't really deserve being called manna, would it? But anyhow, seeing the first head eat this piece of manna, and how it wasn't offering to share the goods like a good head should, the second head got super jealous. It thought, *I'll show that head*, which sure enough it did. Lickety-split the jealous head found a piece of poison fruit and—*gulp!*—ate it right down. Now, you can conjure for yourselves what happened then, girls, I'm pretty darn sure of that. Yes sirree, that jealous head had no sooner eaten the poison fruit than right away it died, both heads, I mean, *the whole bird*, I mean. Wow."

"That is *such* a downer!" The Ecdysiast said.

Her consternation hadn't budged. With furrowed brow she peered toward the diving birds, but they were gone. Stars twinkled pale in the north and east, yet the skies above the silhouette of ridge were still a navy sheet, faintly opalescent. Silence had settled across the camp. Sounds in the distance acquired clarity and mass—a creaking door, a coughing man, the tintinnabulation of water from the window of a cottage through the trees. A blossom swirled before me, and I sighed.

"But *both* of the heads," I suggested, "were beautiful."

"Who cares?" The Ecdysiast said. "I mean, yeah, that's really cool and all, but no matter how gorgeous they were, they're both *dead*." She fixed me with an expectant gaze, as if her meaning were plain. "Silly," she said, "have you ever seen a dead bird dance?"

"Wow, Jenny," Merle said. "I see. You've got a point there, all right."

The Ecdysiast leaned back, lazily running a finger down her stomach. "It's really nice sometimes to know you're not alone," she said.

"Yeah, and on the shiny side of things," Merle said, "probably I'll bet that bird, the one with the two heads, probably it's just dancing somewhere *else*."

"I hadn't thought of it that way," The Ecdysiast said.

"Perfect," I said. "Now we can *all* get a good night's sleep."

"Boy oh boy, did you ever say it!" Merle was absolutely beaming. "A guy hears talk as good as this, with all this joy and truth and so forth, and it clears his mind right out—whoosh!—clean as that old whistle, if you catch my meaning, ready for as peaceful a snooze as ever you could want. But hey, wow, don't let me forget, I'm sure you guys haven't, huh, I'm the only kook round these parts silly enough for that brand of goofery, right, but anyhow, we've got that shindig to go to, Wolfgang and Usch's, remember? Because let me tell you, those two crackpots put on one doozy of a fondue all right, and that's sort of understating it or maybe flipsidelike even gilding the lily or some such thing, hooo-wee girls let's get out of here!"

We arrived at the cottage of our swinging Dutch hosts to find it and the woods all around swamped with the camp's every guest, if not plus a score or two of locals, drunken, stoned, or plain old loony as Wolfgang and Usch themselves.

A quintet of jazzmen drummed and blew their melodious cacophony in the gleam of many torches, as comfortable in their nudity, it appeared, as the rest, and I wondered how the Hollanders had come by these men and, more, how they'd managed to lure them to the camp.

Pling, plong, plung, plong, plung, plong, pling, went the vibes. *Hoom, hum, whoor, hum, whoor, hum, hoom,* cooed the horns beside them. And then in unison the horns leapt up with a *laaaaa di da da di laaa da di!,* clarinet and trumpet, while in the brief, offbeat aftermath the drummer bent to his snare—*rat tat tat tat tat!*

The reedman's fingers danced on his buttons, trilling then lingering, sporadic and smooth by turns. He wrenched his horn, he stroked and lashed and coaxed it. There were geese in his horn, and operatic divas, and grunting titans and bickering crows, and brats and trolls and doves—so much, so much—there was water in his horn, and storms of fire, and raging kleptomaniacs. Behind the man the music went on, intimating, improvisational, the bassist now plucking, now bowing, drums and vibes working one off the next, the whole of their music giving sadness eyes to weep, joy mouths to laugh, anger and fear hands, teeth, and feet to slash and to run, to gnash and beat and tear. That we guests hadn't been swept up in the folds of this art's inexplicable cape seemed a tragic fluke.

I stepped into the crowd.

Glitter did spring from the eyes around me, and laughter from the mouths, arms swung and hands caressed, digits pointed, digits pinched, digits snapped and tapped, skin shimmered, and voices purred, cackled, sighed, and cracked.

But so far as I could see, none of these signs revealed a fascination with the music itself, nor, for that matter, with the men who made it.

At first I was startled by this seeming disinterest. Then I thought, *This is nothing new. It's all being taken for granted.*

Like the lamps in the trees or flowers festooned between them, the musicians were for the folks gathered here but another accoutrement, to be seen, if anyone cared to look, not like fruit at the market or a face in the mirror but through the lens of an ethnologist's distant curiosity, to be heard, which isn't to say *listened to*, through the filter of a constant, if constantly merry, distraction, of which, by the by, the music they played was an ironically important part. Merle alone had remained at my side.

"Who *are* they?" I said.

"You just about know them all as well as I do by now,"

Merle said. "The ones I actually know. Lots of new faces I see this evening, lots of newcomers all right."

"No," I said, waving to the band. "*Them.*"

"Oh, yeah, right, *them.* Well, Wolfgang meets all kinds on the job, taking pictures, that is, what with his being a photographer and such. You've seen him by the pool snapping away, haven't you, the way he pesters all the girls, the perv, or wow, maybe you haven't, I keep on forgetting you haven't actually been out till today, but he does that, for kicks, I mean, Wolfgang, when he's not hauling in the ducats toiling for the magazines and record companies and stuff. That's how he knows these guys. You know these guys?"

"Not even a tad," I said.

"Derrick Rolphy? You've never heard of Derrick Rolphy?"

"Wait a second," I said, the name sounding somehow familiar. "Not *the* Derrick Rolphy."

Merle squinted, his eyes twinkling. "Didn't I say you were one of the golden few?" I watched, incredulous, the musicians lurch and sway. "So then you're a jazz fan, too, I take it."

"Not exactly a *fan*, though I do like it. Clarence used to listen to it often enough. I've still got one of his records even, Rolphy's, I mean, now that I think of it."

"Yeah?" Merle said.

"I forget what it's called. Something about a hunch or bunch or maybe brunch?"

"Yeah, yeah," Merle said, excited. "That's his biggie, *Trout for Brunch.* Pretty nifty, huh, pretty cool? The guys with him now," he said, "are from that same session, all but one. Robbie Kutcherson, Bill Anthony, Teddy Fubbard, the same exact guys, if you can believe it. Dick Mavis, though, the thumper Derrick likes to cut with, he tours like crazy, so he's not here, as if that's really some huge loss, though, heh, because you know who that is there?"

"The ghost of Malcolm X?"

"Tim *Harr*ison, silly, one of the all-time greats, maybe not as good as Mavis or Kingus or them, but still, a real hall-of-famer."

"We really are some of the golden few. Who could've known?"

They'd seen me now and begun to approach the way they had the day I'd abandoned myself to my *self* and, naked, stepped into their snooping arms. Even now their demeanor was weird, the manner of old friends united.

"Rachel," said a rotund man swilling ale from a stein, "glad to see you back again. Looking solid!" He nudged the woman beside him, mousy and thin with lopsided breasts. "Check out the tan action," he said.

The woman laid a hand on my shoulder. "You must've scammed on that recipe in the card we slid you, for your skin!" she said. "You're pretty psychedelic, all right."

"Way to go, Willow," Merle said. "That ointment of yours is out there, definitely, a super-toning, tan-whamming potion if ever I saw one, sure, you'll have to tell me where you scored it some time!"

We tried to move on, but were waylaid by the Arabian who seized my hand and kissed it. "Praise be Allah," he said, rubbing my palm, "that you are well now and come

126

once again among the bounties of this world. I can only hope that my humble offerings pleased you?"

"Yeah, hey there Fakih, good to see you, too," Merle said. "That poetry and the dates you brought over and so forth, they were swell."

"Yes," I said, somehow feeling the need to say something *hip*. "Rumi's lyrics are very, ah, farmed out," I said, "if you follow my meaning."

"Insignificant as shadows," Fakih said as he bowed, "in the light which you cast, Rachel. Scarcely worthy of a glance from your radiant eyes. That you found my gifts to your satisfaction, however, is a blessing to me. The dates, by the way," he said, quite solemnly, "are specially cured. They are for your pleasure during the coming month of Ramadan, if, I mean to say, you have not already indulged in them."

He gazed at me with vulpine intent. I didn't understand. It wouldn't have counted either way, though, I saw, for all at once, hands on his stomach, the man leaned back to explode with laughter.

"Ha ha ha ha ha ha ha! Do you not think that is funny? Ha ha ha ha ha!"

Fingers brushed my shoulder, then—two women, luminous each as swelling moons, were floating in the night before me.

The first was a brunette with feathered bangs, and eyes, green, that were sleepy and alert. Around her waist was a chain of silver dipped in a V at whose tip hung a peridot shaped like a heart.

Beside her, in watery levitation, bobbed a strawberry

girl, her hair a surge of ringlets and waves that fell past her buttocks, four feet long at least. Her beauty was so astonishing that at first I didn't notice the infant in her arms, seemingly asleep, it was so calm. But a closer look showed the child suckling at its mother's breast with an air that, were it older, you could almost have said was demure. Still, the way the child's mother looked, nothing could've been more appropriate or, for that matter, natural. Her mouth was a dolorosa smile.

And they smelled of tea, these women, and of lemon and verbena.

I felt peace, even happiness, surge through me, a sense of gratitude I couldn't place.

"Hey, Rachel," the brunette said. "Hey, yeah, we know you're partying down and just doing your thing, but we thought it would be cool to just introduce ourselves, if that's okay."

It didn't seem possible, but the moment she began to speak, the woman's face opened up with still more ease and grace. Was she a woman from a dream, or a woman lucidly dreaming?

"Anyways," she said, taking my hand, "I'm Rosalyn, and these are my friends Blonda and Jomar Jr."

"Jomar?" I said, gaping.

Till now, I'd believed nothing I was told about that man's doings would come anymore as a shock, not after what I'd seen of him, but, yet again, wonder got the best. It was likely, I thought, that Jomar had entire broods that, at this very moment, were aping their tiny brother.

Blonda murmured as she stroked the child's head.

"So it hasn't been too hard, has it? The scene and the sun and all, getting used to it, I mean?"

"At first it was," I said. "The sun. If it weren't for Merle here, I don't know what I'd have done."

"Yeah, hey, isn't he *mar*velous?" said Rosalyn, and pinched a love handle on my new friend. "Marvelous Merle, that's what we all call him."

"You guys," Merle said.

"Did you tell her, Merle," Blonda said, "we were the ones who sent her that umbrella with the cherries?"

"Ah-oh," Merle said. "Gosh," he said. "Wow. I hate to say it, I really don't want to disappoint you, but you know everyone here's been so wonderful and all and there were so many wonderful gifts and everything that, I don't know, it kind of just slipped by the wayside. Do you think I'm a bogue now?"

"You're so busted," Blonda said.

"But for real," Rosalyn said, caressing my arm. "From the looks of it, Rachel's been taking care of some *serious* business. Who needs shade when you've got a tan like that? Because you've definitely got to be at least as gold as us."

"Not to interrupt here," Merle said, "or change the subject or anything, but I was just wondering if any of you are as hungry as I am? Wolfgang and Usch went to all sorts of trouble to put on a spread, and if this isn't some kind of whopping spread, well then, hey, you can call me Merle the Moron!"

"Hey, yeah," said Rosalyn. "I'm majorly famished."

"Let's go skonk!" said Blonda.

And with that we moved toward the feast. The Lotion

Lady Willow and her ale-swilling man had already made their way to it, as had Fakih with his roaring laughter. *Ha ha ha ha ha ha ha!*

We found The Ecdysiast on a bench between Jomar and Jack. If now and then she deigned to acknowledge the latter, it was with the patience of a guest an ill-mannered dog.

No wonder.

Two hours hadn't passed since Jack had appeared before us with a jug of white gas and threatened to burn his penis.

There we were, nursing our drinks beneath the vines, when Jack burst through a hedgerow, begging The Ecdysiast to acknowledge the love they'd shared.

How else, he'd cried, holding his awful member, on the verge of a speech he could only have memorized, it was so absurd, *can I prove my total head trip for you than by roasting this, my own trippindicular club of horniness, the very one that you, O most wretched of chicks, have without even some bogus excuse chosen to like callously abandon, like it wasn't even a moldy little toke's worth of spleef. Because seriously, dude, my high for you is so out there that if you perchance won't jump back all full of wetness and heat then I am totally worthless. And if that's how it is, so, too, then, O bodacious hag, is my dode totally worthless. It's cool. I mean, you know, checking it out that I'm being so righteously slammed, then before you and all these other dudes I am forced to redress that nevermore shall I use this sad gorilla to climb your fruitful tree and, you know, enact as we once did that highest expression of radical entombment. Adieu, cold dame, I bid you sayonara!*

It goes without saying that for Jack to hazard such a dangerous limb required he abandon the pretense that The Ecdysiast was merely his cousin.

In all likelihood, he'd chosen this particular moment to ambush her because he knew Jomar had gone to town, and he might not get another.

It didn't take long to see this wasn't some awful joke. I suggested Jack take up a lounge and enjoy a drink, what a beautiful evening it had turned out to be, I said, the birds had settled, the planets were winking, real beauty was on the make, come on, sit down, spin a yarn or sing a song. But he wouldn't have the least of it, wrapped up in his fit.

I watched The Ecdysiast watching him, I watched her emotions swell and surge.

This, I knew, was a woman capable of more than a ditzily erudite speech on the finer points of eros and dancing. She knew anger, this woman, she knew scorn, and how to dole them out with an arctic hand. Jack had crossed the line and was now a menace.

Or so once again it seemed. His speech ended without our having signaled any protest or dismay, it was reasonable enough to assume he'd now make good his threat. But our apathy had caught him gullible. No doubt he'd expected something more than what we offered, a scrap of protest, at the very least, though really anything would've done—a whimper, a frown, the bat of a dampened eye. He needed something to hold onto, after all, to bolster his resolve, if ever he'd had it, some threadbare napkin of confidence to keep him on his foolhardy path.

But for Merle, who'd snuck round the cottage to

waylay Jack, we'd done nothing more than watch him from repose.

Our lethargy was for him the crack of doom.

In a flash, the entirety of his pain was manifest—the droop of his eyes, the whole of his invertebrate mien—what more could we need? His threat was pointless because he saw we didn't care what he did with his penis or anything else. And yet all the same he couldn't escape with his honor intact till he'd made the motions of a show.

He opened the jug and held it over his penis. But instantly with this gesture he saw he'd forgot what he couldn't prevail without: the means to make a flame.

The Ecdysiast noted this and sipped her drink with an air of cruel indifference. She was Kim Novak now, scheming, Barbara Stanwyck reaching cat-eyed for her pistol in the pillows of her husband's couch. Her smile whispered calm, but her eyes screamed a wrath to make of Jack's a squealing mouse.

"So come on already, Jacky," she said, "whip it out?"

Her voice had changed, but not. To have heard her, you'd say she was asking Jack to roll up a doobie or crack a bottle of wine. But my ear heard the malice beneath the ditz, the rage and perhaps the hatred. She was enjoying this moment, The Ecdysiast was, and who on Earth could blame her. Here was the mathematics of power, a fortuitous confluence of events the long and short of which said, *It's my way or the highway now, baby, dig?*

"You don't think I'm serious, or what?" Jack said, noticeably wavering. "Cause I shit you not, I'm totally, *totally* serious."

It seemed best to humor the man. Merle had got behind Jack, now, and was quietly approaching.

"Of course you are," I said. "Only we were just hoping you might reconsider . . . well, what you're about to do. There could be some *real* consequences, Jack. Don't tell me I have to paint a picture."

Things couldn't get more pathetic, it seemed, but Jack began to sob. Openly, right on the spot, he collapsed in a fit of tears.

"How could you do it?" he said. "I mean, I thought we were like soul mates. I thought we were hardcore, you know?"

The Ecdysiast touched my hand. "Can you believe what a wuss he's being?" she said. "*Gosh.*"

"This is such a burn, and you know it. You totally fragged me, Jenny. I hope you can live with yourself."

"Excuse me," Merle said.

It didn't matter how calm or easy the words, Jack whirled round agape.

"Oops!" Merle said. "Pardon me, I didn't mean to scare you or anything, sorry, that's the last thing I'd want to do right now, make you feel like you're one of those big old bags of Mexican jumping beans, I just wanted to know if you needed anything while I was inside, a drink or something or maybe a soda or some juice before the big fondue."

He'd placed a hand on Jack's shoulder, a gesture whose effect, like a mystic balm, was immediate. A palpable ease poured through my old "beau," precisely the window Merle had wanted to engineer, during which, pick-pocket smooth, he relieved the man of his jug of gas. Jack had not a clue. On the face of it, he was hypnotized: Merle took the gas, Jack's arm went limp, that was all.

"Or, I don't know," Merle continued, "maybe you just need a hug. What do you think? Come on, Jack, what do you say, why don't you give old Merle here a hug, yeah, that's right, hugs are usually fairly good for this type of situation, where you feel sort of uptight maybe, a little trapped even, I know, I've been right where you are lots of times, believe you me, it'd take me a good three or four days to explain it all, but then you'd get pretty bored I imagine, and anyway a hug will do you real good right about now, what do you say?"

Jack must've known he had no other choice. He fell sobbing into Merle's arms.

"That's good," Merle said. "Don't hold back now, just let it flow, you don't have to worry about anything else but this right now, that's right, you're doing real good, Jack, because you know there isn't anything else right now but what's right here, it's pretty incredible really, just *this*."

The Ecdysiast had had her moment, her fancy had been met. Jack's defeat had pleased her, clearly, and yet she seemed disgusted. She looked at me with her mermaid's eyes and haunted smile, and without a word slipped into the dark.

By now Jack had settled down and was listening to Merle with more than a little attention.

"Everything," Merle said, "is the way it's supposed to be, Jack, if that makes any sense, though probably it doesn't right now, I can only hope that will happen later, hopefully, probably it will if I know you, because you're a pretty all right kind of guy from what I can see, even though you may not believe that, in fact you might even believe just the opposite. But in any case another way of saying that, I guess, is to say everything seems bad right now only because you don't know it's good! See? The way you feel, miserable maybe or maybe just sad, and I guess fairly lost and lonely, too, I imagine, all of that and such, I guess, sorry, I'm not trying to be presumptuous here but it's just that it's pretty obvious, and plus I know you won't like hearing this either, sorry about that, too, not with what's just happened, but all of that, Jack, all of the way you feel?—well, it's totally beside the point, totally irrelevant, since everything, what you feel, the world around you, is all there is, Jack, it's all *it*, which is as hunky-dory as anything can be, if that makes any sense, crazy as it sounds. You know? Or tell me this. Does a snake have legs, Jack—good luck there, whoa, don't think too hard, fat chance, since a snake with legs wouldn't be a snake but something very different, right? So what I'm getting to here, Jack, is that if this were something else, or even *supposed* to be something else, it wouldn't be *this*! This, I mean, is *it*, Jack, *this*, right now, everything and nothing and anything else you can think of, too, the whole nutso shebang. It's all *nowness*, Jack, all *itness*, see, and it doesn't matter what you think or don't think about it because none of it's going to change, no matter what, it's all imperfectly perfect!"

Jack couldn't not have heard these things, they couldn't not have made sense to him on some level, however distant or dim. As Merle spoke, he guided Jack

135

toward the lounge opposite mine and gently set him down. His bearded face was slack with wonder and fatigue, yes, a quality of befuddled sobriety had crept into his features, the expression of a man stepped from his nine-month cave.

Now there was only silence.

From way away on some distant road we heard the purr of a truck as it moved toward a supper-ready home or perhaps instead a factory whose doors it wouldn't see till the early hours of next-day's night.

Closer by, there came the uncking of a squirrel.

You could hear the wings of moths in the vines, you could hear the rush of water on the cans being washed behind the Wagon, through the trees and across the lawn, the sighs, too, of the boy with the hose above them, it seemed—it was just that quiet—the scrape of forks on knives and lids on pots and pans, the simmering cans of corn, the chops a-frying, the softly hissing spuds.

You could hear a child's far-off whimpering, discomfited maybe by the sand in her crotch, weary with the hours of her fun, the murmured croon of a man on a radio, Engelbert Humperdinck or maybe Andy Williams.

It was so quiet, in fact, you could hear the friction of smoke on the gathering dark, of its rising from the pits, slither, slither, thither and thence, the steady trudging as well of ants in their line in the soil between a crack in the stones on the path, the motes of earth beneath their constant legs, the sound, even, above, of the night itself, settling down like the breath of a woman on her sweetheart's eyes.

"That's all really cool," Jack told Merle, awake as ever

I'd seen him, though clearly he was sleeping, "but what if suddenly you found out that God just didn't love you anymore? How do you think it'd make you feel? Pretty shitty, I bet, man, pretty bunk."

"But Jack," Merle said, "that's what I've been trying to tell you. You keep acting like God is a pot of gold someone said you could find somewhere else, and sure, I can understand how that would get you sweaty, all worked up and crazy even, I really can understand, it's pretty normal I suppose. But so then you up and ran off looking for this very heavy pot of gold, but, darn it, you just couldn't find it. Now that could be pretty understandably upsetting, I know, really I do, let me tell you. But what about this? What about all of a sudden this same someone who told you there was a pot of gold out there, I mean what if he went and said, Hey, Jack, you know what, it was all a joke, *hardy har har*, there wasn't ever really a pot of gold, not the way I said at least, and so what with your not having looked so hard, and without ever a glimpse or hint of it, you believed what you'd been told, and gosh darn it, just went and *gave up*? But wait, okay? For the sake of argument, say, what if I happen to come strolling down the way and tell you that all along, the whole time, zany I know, this pot of gold you've heard so much about has been right here, right under your own two feet? What about that, Jack? Well, it's true. *Really*. You don't have to go any further. You can stop right now and be filthy dirty blown-away rich, with all the gold you could ever wish for even in a dream in a movie. And you know what else, Jack, I mean,

I'm sorry here, I don't mean to drag you out, but guess what? You can take *that* to the bank."

"How many times do I have to tell you?" Jack said, and glanced my way, somewhat sheepishly it seemed—though only somewhat, since quite obviously he'd ceased pretending we were more to each other than a user and the boob he'd used. "Jenny's my God, man, or pot of gold, or whatever you want to call it, and she just left me for some Jesus-freak slime ball with tits full of rings."

Some time passed before I realized it had happened, a day or so actually, maybe three, but my anger toward Jack, my ache somehow to avenge myself for the wrongs I believed he'd done me, well, they vanished like shadows with a setting sun.

I saw Jack for what he was, then, in his fragility, in the face of his nameless fear. And once I'd seen this, strange as it sounds, I couldn't help but to love him. I loved Jack then not as a lover loves another but as one who's suffered loves the one who's suffering still.

Jack was living his danger. He was running with the beasts of this world, the maddest dogs and wildest horses, believing, somehow, that this was good for him, that though they were killing him softly, as they say, these beasts were his friends.

All this before we got to the fondue party, what, unbelievably, shameful as it is to admit, I'd virtually forgotten by the time we arrived, given the moil of people, sounds, and smells, the oneiric quality of light and dark, the shimmering of the torches on the trees, plus also of course Derrick Rolphy and his quintet as they pulsated,

joyful and ceaseless, this tune to that, one to the other—
rivers to lakes, and lakes to seas, seas to skies, then skies
again to mountains.

We were here, now.

Now was what there was, *now* was all there was, and it
was just as well I'd let slip from my mind that moment with
Jack—his foolery, so sad, his rejection, the compassion
of Merle—all a fleeting memory, gorgeous as all, in each
of memory's rippling shades, vanishing absent arrival.

We were here, now.

Now I was here.

This was all there was.

The tables were laden with the stuffs of feasts, the
wine and cheese of fondue heaven every way you turned.
Rosalyn and Blonda had remained at our sides, with Jomar
Jr., too, Derrick Rolphy *et al* playing on, driving really, in
mind-meld symbiosis.

Now *their* nakedness was something to behold. They
were naked, but they could just as easily have been Textiles
extraordinaire. Who they were, how they looked, where
they'd come from, their mothers and fathers, brothers,
sisters, wives, friends—none of it counted a blink. What
counted was their music, what they were doing, now, right
there, right then.

Wow.

The fires were flowers, the flowers were song.

What was happening?

How had I got here, and why?

I didn't understand. I did not understand!

But then I did, or something like it. To understand

a thing, the thought of understanding itself has first to vanish, together with the mind that understands. Understanding, I saw, is never any more than the shadow of the thing understood.

And then Merle took my hand.

"I practically just about forgot, Rachel," he said, having seen our companions, "what with all these beautiful interruptions and so forth, but Jomar said he had something for you. Jomar!" he said. "Hey there, buddy, hey, look who's here!"

"All right, Midnight!" shouted Jomar. "And my foxy jiggle show, too, resurrected at last, and Rosy and Blonda even, and holy holies, my *boy*. Out of sight, man, come on over, guys!"

The Ecdysiast may not have known Jomar had women wherever he went, and children by them, too, in nameless sums. This could well have been the first time she'd heard such news. I watched her with such joy in her eyes, such laughter and glee, and I could tell she didn't care. She didn't care where Jomar had been or what he'd done, with whom or when. She was happy with him, now, she had no expectations of him, now, everything by golly was all right by her.

Jomar stayed put, but The Ecdysiast leapt up and wrapped me in her arms. And rich she was with patchouli, fire, smoke, piney and clean, and happy, too, if smoke can be said to be happy, and with earth, as well, she had a woodsy, leafy, grassy old scent, as thick as if she'd stepped from a tubful of bottomland earth, and with these the flavor of cheese and bread, and the odor of wine, and the odor of kirsch, and tarragon, lemon, mustard, and sage, steaming and simmering with meat and cheese, all of it about her and all about us, the smell of her inside and about me, in my mind—she was in my mind!

And The Ecdysiast was tittering. Not the tittering I'd since disdained with such malice, I admit, but a tittering that had nothing to do with mindlessness and the world to do with wonder and glee, a most wonderful tittering, so wonderful a way. It was her laugh is what, unabashed as a lark in a meadow singing to an exultation, unabashed as love, all of a piece, like the music round us, now, her laughter had become a part of that music, she herself was music.

Strange girl! Dancing girl! Laughing, flying, gleeful girl!

How could you not have been infected with the joy she had to give? How could you not have helped but to swell before it so pure? It was as impossible as a finger pointing to its tip.

Gosh, she said, you won't believe it, she said, the food was *so* fantastic, she felt as though she'd been eating for days, she didn't care what happened to her body, nothing could bum her out tonight, and gosh, where had I been and why so long, though that was cool, whatever it was, the vibes were cool, everything groovy, what was there to trip on when you had your friends about you and plenty for the whole, she said, it's so totally gorgeous, she said, just wait till you taste it, hurry, hurry, sit down here, we've saved you a place, and you'll never believe what Jomar got, you'll love it, Rachel, I'm sure, I'm so glad you're here!

My heart was a room that could never be filled. I was a room to roam forever, whose bounds you could see but like rainbows not obtain, fast or far though you ran.

"Now close your eyes?" The Ecdysiast said, and led me round the table. "Okay, and when you open them, Jomar will give you a big surprise?"

"Dig it, Rachel," I heard Jomar say. "Are you ready for this?"

"I can't stand it," I said.

"But seriously, though, are you ready to get blown away?"

"You're killing me already," I said.

"Then open your eyes, foxy lady, and check it out."

A woman, blonde and tan, with faint though definite lines at her eyes, was gazing into mine, a face if studied that could offer little or explode with tales of love and woe, of days in a life of mystic potions and dusty tomes, failed incantations whispered in shuttered rooms.

It was an ordinary face, and yet somehow stunning, not for a reason, no single part evoked real beauty, beauty as it's typically told. In its essence, this was where the beauty lay, a beauty absent parts—no thesis, antithesis, synthesis, none.

I saw this face, I gazed into this face, blinking as it blinked, but for my life, I couldn't say whose it was.

"Now is that a foxy lady," Jomar said, "or is that a foxy lady?"

And then, with a great swelling rush, like the rush at the start of a squall at sea, I understood with delight and terror that this face before me, enigmatic and divine, belonged to the thing I'd always called *me*.

It was my own face I gazed into, though maybe it wasn't, in truth I knew nothing, how could I?

But whomever it belonged to, this face, another or me, it was the face of the face in the mirror Jomar had placed before it, my gift from him, fantastic.

I had no voice to struggle with, then, I'd been abandoned by my voice. The smallest sound was past me—gone—my voice was dead and gone. I felt sick inside. I felt wonderful and scared, I felt so very sick.

My vision shut down, dark and light had swallowed the world, everything spinning, the world was spiraling formless *stuff*.

Nor could I breathe, nor hear, I couldn't see or speak or breathe or hear, nor even feel, nothing but nausea, I'd been consumed, and lost.

I'd been dropped, it seemed, into the everyday of my self—of my everyday feelings, my everyday comprehensions—the reservoir of the great untapped quotidian, absent the way to know them in the least.

Terror, joy, anger, rage, boredom, loathing, bliss—they were there, and but a few, each of them strange, none of them, in other words, *mine*.

I was a stranger to my *self*, as if, almost, the person I was were a painting I'd never seen, or perhaps seen too much, who could say, a poem perhaps read one too many times.

The face before mine was hauntingly familiar, while nothing about it made a scratch of sense.

I was lost, I was nothing, no longer a person, I knew, or even a thing, what I was was *not*.

And then with the same swelling rush of the moment before, sick in every cell, I disintegrated, left to myself, the woman I thought I'd known but hadn't, then or ever.

I began to cry.

And the thing is, I didn't shed merely tears, I didn't merely moan, but wept as never, as I'd never thought a person could weep, as never a person could weep without dying, the weeping of a woman who'd seen her death then stared into her face on its bier.

Then they returned, these coldly foreign feelings, now possessed of terrible heat. Overwhelmed, so all at once dazed, I collapsed at the table heaving.

And then I was on my feet, stumbling through faces and groping limbs, shadow, light, fire, earth . . .

Pictures rushed at me like spirits from the black near sleep—a pot of bubbling cheese, a man's big toe, a nipple, a leaf, a cleaver on a board on a table of cleavers and boards, forks and knives and meats . . .

Two hands, disembodied, rose before me and flapped away . . .

A branch slashed my face, windows winked through trees . . .

Vodka plagued my nostrils and tongue, and the acid from a belch, as Sonny and Cher croaked lines from their famous song . . .

I saw fire in the distance. Bodies moved behind it, shadows on a wall . . .

And then a meadow, then I was stumbling over roots through trees . . .

Water flowed round my ankles, my thighs, I felt moss at my toes, I'd entered a creek, I was slipping on slippery rocks . . .

And then I fell in the water, and I let the water take me.

Over rocks and logs I floated, slack in the current, bright with cold, my body adrift in a deep black pool, the wheeling of stars above.

How I'd got there meant nothing. I knew only that I was there and sentient once again.

How cold the water was! How clear my mind, how empty!

From either side rose a wall of trees. An ermine appeared on a bank, maybe ten feet off, and paused on a stone to watch. It stayed put as I moved toward it, perched on its stone unblinkingly, and then I was crouched before it. And as I raised my hand, it raised its chin to bare its throat, and then it turned and vanished.

I rose from the water.

I stepped to the bank.

I felt dirt at my feet, pebbles, twigs, and stones.

I set my hand on a tree.

I smelled its sap.

I scraped moss on a rock and heard the mewling of raccoons.

Then a tiny owl slipped through the trees, it came and it went, embarrassed and amazed I watched the owl, I let the owl be so.

And then I knew I was cold, I fathomed the cold, wonderful and utter. I stood in that feeling, I plunged into my feeling, I embraced the cold as it had me.

And then back through the trees, back through the field, to the tang of food and whir of speech, surely though calmly I strolled through the world—it would be when I came or if not it wouldn't. The night was the night, and so till the sun had risen to make it day.

Things once nebulous were now precise—volleyball nets, an exercise bike, a chain-link fence round a pool at the core of beach balls, tables, rafts, and chairs.

An old bald man with saggy buttocks and hairy hands skimmed leaves off the pool with a net.

A crew of rabbits crossed my path.

A light went out in a cabin.

I strolled past the tennis courts, the Chuck Wagon, too, sleepily forlorn with its shuttered windows and gated doors. A band of crickets played from the roses, and then the club house, too, appeared, its things more useless beneath the lights, a wordless lament, a confession—*Look, see, there's no one here, there's no one here to see or hear, we were waiting, is all, for someone to come, and you'd know if someone had, though they haven't, no one's here, not anyone's here, all of us, so meaningless without you . . .*

I stepped into the sand of the playground, I mounted the carousel and spun myself round. The swing set, monkey bars, see-saw, and slide, all of them motionless, all of them empty, waiting for the kids of tomorrow.

The spinning went on, steady but slow—the swing set, monkey bars, see-saw, and slide, round and round, these things I'd seen so many times at school, five days a week for ten long years but knew nothing of, these things for play of the world's Abel Riches and Rhonda Lynns.

Rhonda Lynn! Abel Rich! Sad blue girl! Frightened nasty boy!

And I, who could only have added to the sadness and fear of that petrified boy by tearing out his hair for no reason more than that I was frightened and sad myself, than that I myself had been so blue, than that, somehow, for a single heated instant, I'd perceived him, a boy, as the symbol and source of all my pain, the man inside the little boy, the boy inside the little man, every man who'd done me wrong, whom I'd observed to have done me wrong, harmed me with cruelty, harmed me with indifference, who like Jack when he wasn't indifferent was mushily sweet just to reach his ends, who, like Jack, had lied from illusory beginning to illusory end, salesman that he was, shabby human that he was, may the world forgive me my crimes against them and against the boy expressly, might it forgive them, too, what they'd done and were doing and might do more of yet in their days to come.

The carousel had stopped.

My feet were in the sand, dusty, I knew, though I couldn't see it, the dust on my naked feet. I knew only the feeling of dust on my feet. The cottages slumbered across the way. I could hear the sound of merriment past them, and of music, and of laughter, and of brilliant hurrahs, one on the next and next.

The coldness had left me, now it was warm, pretty nearly balmy the air had become, I'd entered a mild sweat. My feet were sticky with dust and sweat, my ankles and calves were sticky. And I saw again, now, as if anew, that I was utterly naked.

147

Seeing this again, myself anew, my breasts as they were, my belly with freckles and one small mole, my tuft of hair, my calves and toes, I felt suddenly, what, very, very *good*.

And how in the world could that be?

This wasn't an ordinary sense of contentment, either, a sense of happiness with my state. It was the feeling of acceptance, and the feeling of goodness in it, a deep true knowing I was good as I was, I'd never need more to continue on, to know always and ever I was good as I was—ha!—*I was good as I was.*

How had this happened? How had I lived never having seen myself before?

It was Merle. Or rather it *wasn't* Merle, or rather again it was what Merle had *not* made me do, *not* made me be.

Merle hadn't *made* me feel good, but in his gentleness *shown* me how to feel good myself, shown me with his gestures and words that such a way was there to be had. He, after all, had done it, was doing it, he after all was living his truth, knowing he was good and loving himself for who he was and wasn't, that was so terrifically apparent— yes—he'd shown past doubt that the self he saw in me was the self I'd not once seen in all those desperate years. Not even Clarence—despite what I'd believed to have been his own kind goodness—had been able to do this, to give me the gift of myself.

And I knew what I had to do.

I had something to do!

Most of the party had gathered up front with the fires and music and food. And there were more people, now, too, than when I'd left, a packed mass of revelers so high on themselves and life they'd begun to emanate a tangible glow of fun and maybe something even transcending fun, what through a kind of synergy had boomed to a living net of, what, I don't know, *beatitude*.

But it was the capers to the rear that really nabbed my eye.

I was swallowed instantly by dread, and with it the memory, old, of my parents on a rock by a river, become, as the Bard once so famously declared, the beast with two backs.

Dread was my feeling, yes, dread had captured my essence, too, and yet powerful though it was, it seemed as well beyond me, more the *memory* of dread than dread itself.

Revoltingly curious, or curiously compelled, or compellingly revolted, whatever it was, I'd been taken, helpless to repent, despite the voice that urged me, and I went on.

From the line of trees, where the fire's glow had faded enough to see unseen, I peered out to find that—wow!—

as Merle would say, my hunch had been *right on the money*. And ghastly as it was to witness this sight, witness it I did.

In the dirt by the fire lay a man in full recumbence, his youthful penis stout as a post and his face incognito beneath a moaning Usch. As for that old crow, she sat astride this man, turning her spotted hips with a sort of automatic prowess while with her own mouth and hands she mechanically yet furiously toiled at the penis of the man on his feet before her—this was indeed another— who was himself, by God it's true, wrenching away at Wolfgang's own, which, repulsively, there beneath the paunch of his hairless gut, had remained for all the young man's efforts flaccid as a popped balloon.

Wolfgang no doubt had found it necessary to compel this partner of his into a dribble of potty-talk nonsense, the young man hailing the old, more or less, for the sleek masculinity on show now that Wolfgang had shaved away his pubic hairs!

It should go without saying that this fellow was obliging his partner with plenty of mustard and onions, yammering away to the tune of *Ah dude, you're so hot, did you know that, oh yeah, man, really, fuck, you're so fucking hot, I mean, hey, Mary, would you check out Wolfie's cock, man, I mean that's some serious fucking cock he's got there, he'd probably really dig it if you came over here and set your raging little puss right down on it, you know, yeah that's right, Usch baby, keep it up, yeah, yeah, yeah,* never once missing a beat in the task of ramming himself into Usch's face.

Meantime, on a lounge just a few feet off, the woman the man had been talking to, also rather young and in all likelihood his wife, stretched out in shammed repose, filming this crapulence with a giant camera.

"Usch!" Wolfgang said. "Did you hear these? These are a good idea I believe, to have this beautiful womans Mary perform as Douglas wants to announce. Do you might not think these also?"

"Oh man, dude," said the fellow named Douglas, and grabbed Usch's head, "you *know* she wants to, man. Fuck. She's so fucking hot for you, man. Her cunt's like a fucking boiler room, man, believe you me. Come on over, Mary, and you know, stoke this dude up with that bodacious fucking cunt of yours!"

"I *love* this things," Wolfgang said. "To do this things while I am on this things, such lovely, erotical things! Usch, is it suggested maybe that you should watch when this womans will do these for me?"

Half of what made all this—ugh!—these *acts* so cheap, was how the actors were acting them, with, it seemed, such vulgar calculation. They'd attended to every trapping—these allegedly wild humans engaging their allegedly wild acts, the manic gestures, the hideous talk, the moans and groans of absurd bliss—but only superficially, for their faces were those of robots.

They were robots, yes, goonish and uncouth, and it wasn't love they were sharing but stifling. They were fornicating goons with frozen eyes and vulgar mouths, and nothing they tried or did could veil their hurt and fear, their longing, their shame, assured. And yet they couldn't escape the urge to commit their deeds, to utter-mutter their vulgar words, nor, I imagined—I could've been wrong, I've been

wrong so many times—would they ever feel actual pleasure,
but merely its idea, that they were wanted by more than a
single other—lover, partner, mate.

Wolfgang had thrown himself to the dirt like the
man beside him, the feet of the woman Mary planted
at his sides the better to bounce on his now distended
part. She ignored her husband and with her camera
went about her business.

Endlessly, it seemed, this went on till at last, and to
my huge dismay, Wolfgang looked directly at me.

"Usch!" he said. "Look! There inside these trees, this
is Rachel there amused with her hairs of sun!"

Usch pushed Douglas aside and, the rest of them fixed
in their tableau of ousted poseurs, as if she'd been told I
was a psychopomp, advanced on me in a blind sort of trot.

"Where is this womans?" she shouted. "Rachel, where
did you stay in that forest?"

Before the sight of her in such frantic delight, I
collapsed into sobriety. "Is something the matter, Usch?"
I said, and stepped from the trees.

"The matter is this things I have you for!" she said.
"Welcome, *Ra*chel. You have a very good welcome!" Her
hand found mine and began to knead its fingers. "You
must come there now. Wolfgang and this peoples, they
are ready for you!"

"Thank you *so* much," I said, "but you know what?
Someone at the party has just played a trick on me. I'm sure
you won't believe it. They told me they'd seen a *uni*corn
out here in the trees, and well, silly me, I ran off to look."
Her eyelids working like shutters, her eyes themselves

engulfed by corrupted pupils, the lady squeezed my hand. "Anyhow, please, don't let me interrupt you."

"No!" Usch said, *sotto voce*. "This is the things I want. You see, this mans over there, Douglas, his balls are smelling like an old man's bed. I would not ask for you to do this things I am doing on him there, these are for sure."

I've heard people say what I'd thought impossible, which because I'd discounted them from the realms of the plausible, I believed they couldn't have said. The sheer foulness of the image the woman had just fixed in my mind, the strange aptness of her trope, found me at once sympathetic and disturbed. And yet how much could that count? My confusion was irrelevant. Once again, Usch had spoken.

"Surely not, Usch," I said. "The last thing you are is thoughtless."

In that moment, with her frown, Usch, if such could be, seemed a melancholy apple.

"I am erotical!" she blurted. "Yes, very erotical on this things we have!"

"And don't forget about *thoughtful*," I said. "You're one of the most thoughtful persons I've ever met. Shame on those phonies for spreading their rumors."

From behind his wife, Wolfgang made his way toward us. The others had gathered by the fire to gossip, I presumed, about the rupture in their "games." And now Usch's frown was a shining grin.

"Here comes Wolfgang," I said. "What do you say we bring him round to the front so the three of us can take care of my sneaky friend. For his fib, I mean?"

"These are not what can happens in this places, *R*achel, this kinds of sneaks that are not good to do. No, Wolfie will not agree to these either! Wolfie!" she said. "Hurry, you, we must come with *R*achel to get these mans friend that she has that are suggesting her to things which cannot be true. Hurry, Wolfie, we must come at this same moments!"

Wolfgang's pupils, too, were swollen past repair. It was as though he were looking *through* me, toward a notion reifying in the dark indistinctly behind.

A fear seized me, that little gremlin in the drain scratching to get out.

And then as quickly I knew it wasn't fear I felt but, like my memory of dread the moment before, the memory of fear, or rather the memory of fearing fear, of fearing that I'd once again become invisible, inconsequential, transparent, whatever, as I'd been that night in the Oakland bar.

Wolfgang held out a plastic bag. What I'd taken at first for truffles were mushrooms—*magic* mushrooms— and Wolfgang and Usch had eaten more of them than I could know.

"This is sunny things for you," he said, "as you are sunny. This things are right for everythings which you might have to do, all this erotical things, all this gold things in the suns. You must reach in your hand, *R*achel."

"No, Wolfie," Usch said, and started away. "This is a sneaks in the front, who are suggesting *R*achel to this things about *un*icorns on this nearby trees! We must come there now to know why these sneak is doing this things. Hurry!"

"Sneaks!" Wolfgang said. He, too, had started off in his own blind trot. "Then they must also reach into this sunny things we are holding, do you not confess these with me also, Usch?"

"Hurry, Wolfie!" Usch cried out. "Hurry you, too, *Rachel!*"

The bacchanalians up front had circled the musicians, I presumed—reasonable in light of the '50s tune for strippers they were playing.

The swingers had vanished, done like me and pushed into the crowd.

Naturally I should've known better than to think some new screw hadn't turned, and, more, that my old "beau" wasn't at its heart.

For it wasn't Derrick Rolphy and friends grinding away to that funtime beat, but my very own Jack, and to the crowd's enormous delight. Had this been the first time I'd met him, or seen his awful member, I'd have been shocked—utterly completely. But I *had* met the man, and, so true, far more than I cared to say, I'd seen his awful member. This, on the other hand, wasn't to say I wasn't shocked. I was shocked, all right, and not just *utterly completely*. Jack, Jack, Jack!—my little Jack of Hearts! Nothing was past him, from the depths of trite to the heights of scandal, nothing was remotely past him.

He was prancing round a pile of clothes, a skirt, a blouse, and a bra, from what I could tell, plus also underwear, stockings, and stilettos—patent leather, these last, and bright red.

From where he'd dredged these up I couldn't guess, but, really, who the heck cared? He *had* dredged them up, there they were, and, prancing for a crowd on the edge of frenzy, there he was, all the while, as if none of this could suffice, twirling his penis like a dancer her boa, round and round with the gauche femininity and relish, truly, you'd imagine the hallmark of just that sort of dancer.

The man had even gone so far as to smear his face with makeup—lipstick, rouge, mascara—in the crude approximation not of some burlesque B-girl but a pavement-pounding tramp.

He was, needless to say, hideous, something from a Mario Bava film, *Bay of Blood* maybe or *Twitch of the Death Nerve*, with a face between Claudio Volonté's and Carol Burnett's, covered in hair and gore, fantastically androgynous, fantastically tweaked, his eyes forlorn as the saddest clown's, the birthmark on his cheek pulsing like a beacon, past description, his face, hideous above his crude gyrations, jawing, twisting, pouting.

It was horrible, yes, it was hideous, yes, hideous and horrible and comical, too, and yet for all his awkward grace, and despite his awful whirling member, the figure he presented was undeniably compelling.

I wanted to take my eyes from him, verily I did, more than I'd wanted to flee Wolfgang and Usch in their debauch, but I was for the life of me rooted, clichéd as that may sound, fixed in what I could only describe as horrified composure.

The people around me, however, though no less stunned than I, were far from stricken motionless or dumb. With every switch of Jack's lean hips, with his every grotesque thrust, the crowd hooted and cheered the more. They were laughing, too, and whistling, shouting support, crying praise, championing him, actually, as surely as they would a hero-turned-stripper or stripper-queen.

But wait, I thought. *What was this really, when Jack was* already *naked?*

The clothes before him he had to have shed some time before, though, neatly folded as they were, this didn't seem the case. Had he stripped them off one by one, they'd have been spread around the crowd. In truth, Jack was just getting started.

Yes, and this, it soon grew clear, wasn't a striptease he was performing, but an *anti*-striptease extraordinaire!

I saw The Ecdysiast. Jostled by the crowd, she was bent with rage, from the freckles on her nose to the soles of her dazzling feet, she was fury in a body. Even her hair was furious, jutting out electrically. She was alone in the crowd, for the first time, so far as I could tell, quaking with her fabulous rage, helpless withal as Jack performed his *dance*. Honestly, I wouldn't have been surprised to see the man disintegrate, then, just combust before the hatred in her eyes. Nor would I've wondered to see her collapse in tears. Jack, poor girl, was mocking her!

Yes, this *dance* of his was a mockery, one to end all mockeries for all time, a mockery that rendered The Ecdysiast, together with her love for dancing and its lore, a travesty far past epic.

And this was to say nothing of the travesty it made of dancing itself, of the women who stripped and the men who paid them, and even of the crowd, of every person that made every crowd gathered to every dancer *erotique*, and especially of the crowd before which Jack now danced, strippers themselves, these people, naked as they were, hostile as they were to clothes and the humans who wore them, the Textiles of the world, ignorant to their role in Jack's charade as they cheered him fanatically on.

My God! It didn't seem possible, first, that Jack could've dreamt such a thing or, second, once born, that he could have pulled it off.

In one moment he was twirling the underpants round, in the next, shimmied to the edge of the crowd, face-to-face with The Ecdysiast, no less, writhing in a way you could only call monstrously come-hither. She watched him from her desolation, then broke away and fled.

Jack by God had won, or so by his expressions—the grimace of triumph, the solipsistic hail—he must surely have believed. And with each new switch or thrust, the crowd's roar expanded.

The bassist meantime had been cackling with abandon, repeatedly shouting, *The sneak! The sneak!* till finally he was drained and the band slipped into another, more sultry tune, the sax man grinding out his seduction of oozy notes.

Jack never missed a beat.

The underpants on, he struggled to store his penis there, impossible, clearly, in light of the lack to work with. And they weren't tiny, either, come from one of the fuller ladies with us, a 16-sized gal by the looks. Nor would it have mattered had Jack crammed himself into a pair of shorts. Trying *to commend the poisoned chalice to the lips*, as it were, was pointless with less than pants. With calculated slowness, Jack slid a stocking up, and then again the other. Garters emerged, which he donned with facility enough to convey rehearsal plenty. Then he slipped into the heels, and from there the cheap brassiere, whose cups in glee he stuffed with the grapefruit that had magically appeared. Finally, slithered into his skirt and blouse, my little Jack of Hearts—Textile superb—set to prancing wobbly on the heels while with his unspeakable face he grinned and cooed, the crowd itself singing back in ribald phrases, women and men as one.

And then—*fait accompli*!—the music ceased, the players held out their hands.

Silence held the forest now—we heard flickering torches and treetops in the breeze—only to vanish in applause as the crowd broke round Jack, some ripping pieces from his clothes, like teenyboppers mauling a star.

Quite obviously these people were ensorcelled. Madness reigned, oblivion reigned, the crowd had been laced with elixir of aconite and water from the river Lethe, transformed into connoisseurs of sin.

Beneath this tsunami of stooges, Jack could do no more than stagger. And scarcely had he been hoisted to their shoulders than they expanded, then parted, then of one rabid mind tore off with their hero to the chant of *Do it! Do it! Do it!*

Oddly, despite the attempts of some to strip Jack of his clothes, others rallied to his spirit and adorned him with still more.

They'd actually got the man into a tunic, with over that a poncho. Someone else had stuffed his hair into a snood and arms into gloves, the sort you see on divas through the lights and smoke. Bangles and rings appeared, and a wreath made of willow was pressed onto his head, and his chest hung thickly with necklaces of flowers and hemp.

In seconds Jack had morphed from modern clown to Christmas tree, yucky with the charms of nincompoops and donkeys.

Presently the crowd departed in a line through the trees, chanting and weaving with Jack in his glory, hands above his head.

"Is there by chance anything left for a famished traveler?" I said to Jomar, who'd appeared like a guardian at my side. The mirror he'd given me was on the table still, face down.

"Hallelujah, Foxy!" he said. He held my hand for a moment, as Usch had before, caressing it. "Is it true, that you're all copasetic now?"

"I am hungry, Jomar, as in *starved*."

"I've got to tell you, lady, you tripped us out. We thought—*I* thought, me and Jenny did—that maybe you'd just got some bogus news."

Merle was with us, too. "Have you both been here the whole time?" I said.

"We've been here," Merle said, "and here we are."

"You mean *you've* been here," Jomar said. He turned to me. "This cat was the only one around who didn't go flipping out."

"Did you see Jenny?" I said. "She looked terrible."

"What happened?" Jomar said.

"Poor thing," Merle said, "she could likely use some comfort, if you know what I mean, especially from a swell guy like yourself, I mean most folks can when they get like that, feeble like and so on."

"Don't you two book while I'm gone," Jomar said. "We'll be right back."

I picked up the mirror. The frame was of walnut, and on the back, finished in blue and gold, was the image of a woman who looked like Danaë, caught in repose, her head on a pillow beneath the shower of gold that was Jupiter at her tower.

"A piece of glass," I said. "Gorgeous, I suppose, but still just a piece of glass."

"For some," Merle said. "For you."

I set the mirror on the table, face-up. "Promise you won't tell Jomar?"

"Tell him?"

"That I did this," I said, and smashed the mirror with an empty pot.

Merle's chin doubled. His lips puckered and his eyes bulged.

"*Wow*," he said. "I mean, heck, no, I won't tell him, sure I won't, and wow, that was, how would you say it, heck, *brave*, I guess."

"It really is a beautiful frame. I'll hang it on my wall when I get home."

The fires had died, the flowers had wilted, the music was no more.

All around us lay the night's remains, used and half-used things which without judgment were whole in themselves, I knew, though still somehow funny, somehow sad, somehow, despite, inexplicably gorgeous.

Merle slid over and held me.

He was holding me, and I was holding him.

We were alone, we were, it was all so true: the world was really funny.

Alone together at the cottage at last, Merle and I began to kiss.

To hold each other—how kindly, how gently, how absolutely lovingly—was a thing beyond. But better still was our laughter, it went on and on. The *what* and *how* of things had skipped into the night. I couldn't say *Yea* or *Nay* or even *Bring me a glass of water, Mephistopheles, I'm oh-so-thirsty with all this crazy romance!* And even if I could, it would've surely paled.

The world might have been melting, and I wouldn't have said a word.

And we never did, Merle and I, we spoke not a teensy peep.

We were so far from what I'd have imagined, a love minus platitudes—no bedside kneelings, no eros in verse, no fruit dipped in wine, no sitars, tablas, flutes, just we two, late at night, alone on the couch, wordlessly touching and kissing.

And I had to say, it felt so *good*.

Clarence had never made me feel this way, brought me to such a wondrous place. With him I'd always had the sense of being taught. I wasn't so much his wife, I saw only now, his equal, as his beautifully stumbling student, exquisite to him, perhaps, but never to me myself. However gentle Clarence may have been, however passionate and respectful, I'd always felt I was doing something wrong, I'd always felt through his guidance alone that I'd approached the status, say, of sufficient lover, that without that guidance I was no one and nothing, and would be as such so long as I was without him.

But it was only because of Clarence, I saw, as well, that I could now know this one sure thing: I was loved by Merle Frizzel, Merle Frizzel loved me really and truly.

Not that he'd said as much. He hadn't needed to say as much. And that was how I knew.

Merle was like the sage who, never having made a show of greatness, had reached beyond all greatness. He never contended, never strove, and could therefore never be held in contention.

Just so his love. There it was, unshakably present. Had I nothing else, which I'd come to see, I had love, the love of Merle, Merle was my lover.

And it was this having naught but love that lent the smallest things their power.

But past all the rest, I could now bear not just the bright but gentle force of love, but also the greenest envy, the yellowest fear, the blackest rage and grayest sorrow— anything, really, the world had ever felt. Like Merle, through Merle, I, too, had somehow shed the bottom.

What had happened? How had I been so blessed?

```
♄    9 degrees.
♃   12 degrees.
♂    7 degrees.
☉   17 degrees.
♀    8 degrees.
☿    7 degrees.
☽   12 degrees.
```

And then Jack came crashing in.

He was adorned still in his harlequin motley—the same snood, minus, now, the crown of willows, the same gloves, both muddy and one torn, the same tunic, mud-spattered, too, the same stilettos, minus a heel, the same vulgar makeup, fallen, were that possible, to deeper vulgarity yet, mainly from his tears.

For, yes, the man was weeping now, wailing really—
¡pobrecito!—as if for the catastrophic end.

We learned later that the drugs he'd taken that night included an insupportable quantity of Wolfgang and Usch's "things." Which wasn't to say Jack's grief was a phantom, only that, rather than allay his suffering, the drugs had done their work too well. First they'd provoked his dance—the idea of the anti-striptease, he'd tell us, didn't occur to him till he felt the tug of his "shrooms"—and then, that tickling turned to torment, they exploited his grief and brought it to a pitch.

Now, collapsed on the rug before us, he gibbered on about *what he was going to do*. We tried to calm him, Merle and I, to make sense of his pain, but failed.

Milk, Merle said, was a remedy for mushrooms, but when I brought some to Jack, he flung it down and boiled on in rage.

Finally, in the bathroom, he vomited, then lay back in his mess, glistening with slime, with nothing to purge but his demons themselves.

Make them and *how for* and *going to pay* were as much as we could get from his babble, so we doused him in the shower.

We may as well have set him in a cloud of bees.

The water hit him, and he let go with a shriek, then jolted to his feet.

Seeing him, his face knobby with anguish and surprise, we thought that maybe he'd reached the beginning of the end, that like a beast shot with dope he'd thrash about in his charade of death before collapsing into slumber. Instead, he tore down the curtain, leapt from the tub, and smashed into the door. When it gave but failed to rend, he smashed it again, loosening the hinges, and then again yet, dropping it with a clap.

Merle and I couldn't do more than shrink away, my arms round his neck, Jack all the while howling.

He crashed into the bedroom, banged round the closets and ripped open bags, then rushed out the door with another super clap. The screen squealed slowly shut.

We communed in the forest, Merle and I, at his *place*. There was no cottage, not even a hut, just a mat of straw on the grass at the edge of a glade, beneath a towering spruce.

Beside the mat was a pit where Merle built our fire, and we lay down, no blankets or wraps, just the fire's warmth.

He kissed me, I kissed him back.

He kissed my eyes, I kissed his.

He kissed my neck, I kissed his, he kissed my aching breasts.

I kissed his arms and hands, his fingers one by one, and he kissed mine, my arms, my hands, my fingers one by one.

He kissed my stomach, I kissed his hips.

He kissed my thighs, in and out, I kissed his knees, and the tender skin behind.

And my calves, as well, he kissed them, too, and my feet, and each of my goofy toes, and my fingers combed his hair, and his shoulders I caressed, I held him with my love and hope. And I smelled his smell, and I tasted his mouth and the salt of his unique sweat.

The night was around us, coiling with tresses of mist.

Stars glimmered faintly, strange birds called out, round our own strange calls and cries.

We were there, together, my legs round him like the night round us, as glad as the night, the stars, the trees, the birds.

We were there.

Our love was there.

One woman, one man, we were, alone in our unity, unified in loneness, no longer lonely, and nevermore again.

We had lapsed into sleep. The rain brought us back. I looked into his eyes and kissed his nose.

The glade was still, sleepy with rain, and fresh with light the flowers shone undiminished.

Merle was a gardener. His love for the earth, and mostly for flowers, brought him to this place each night that he wake to it newly with every sun.

A bevy of deer were grazing, six or eight at the line of the trees. Blackbirds gathered in unseen charms, and meadowlarks, too, the song of them melding with the rain.

We were alone. There was no one else, nor the sound of someone else, just a thick magnificence, the ancient trees, the majestic trees, their own song and smell, the rain, welcome as cool and wonderfully refreshing. I thought of no word but *lovely*.

Merle gave me his hand, and we went into the meadow, and we didn't speak for hours.

I was no longer naked, no longer abashed, but nude.

This was not an *ideal*, we were not an *ideal*, something from a bygone idyll or myth.

It was the world.

There was nothing to think of, nothing to say.

This was the *world* we were in, or rather, no, for we were not *in* the world, separate from the things of the world around us, but the world itself.

Yes and yes, we were *worlding*.

I found Jack in a chair at the cottage, his penis, again, in hand.

Something had happened to him, that much was sure, what, he wouldn't say. I greeted him with cheer, like the night before had never been—like, as Jack was later to say, it really had been just an evil dream—though he said no word.

I went to the toilet, which to my astonishment Jack had cleaned and repaired. The door had been fixed, and the rest made right, as well. But Jack wouldn't look me in the face when I returned, he wouldn't so much as move.

"You may or may not be too keen on this," I said, "depending on how you feel, but would you like me to fix you a drink?"

"You'd do that for me?"

I made a tray of gin and tonic and ice and lime and fixed the drink and offered it.

"Courtesy," I said, "of Chez Hill."

Jack tried to smile. Then his gaze found the drink, where for a time it remained queerly fixed.

"Well?" I said.

I thought he hadn't heard me, but then he snatched the drink and gulped it down and without pause dropped to his knees and poured the gin and gulped it down again.

"Nothing like a slurp of juniper juice to spook your woes away," he said.

Color had appeared in his face again. His eyes were shiny and moving round the room in his habit's suspect way.

"Jack," I said, and placed a hand on his knee.

"What's up, Flowerpuss?" he said.

"Have you considered that there's a way out of this?"

He leaned back and scanned the room, as though someone might be in the curtains with a gun or maybe just a camera.

"Since when did *you* become the emcee for *I've Got a Secret*?"

"It wasn't me who brought you here."

Jack proffered his glass and rattled its ice. "How's about another?"

"It's only when you don't believe in people that you make them liars, Jack," I said and mixed his drink. "People turn people into liars every day."

"Like right now even," Jack said. "I mean, that's what you could call me if I told you you didn't need a slurp of this stuff more than me."

"I know you think I'm a fool," I said.

This did something to him. His smile vanished, and his color with it. The whole of his body slipped back into the eel it had been.

"And you know what else? I'm tired of your sweet-talk. My name is Rachel. Yours is Jack."

The alcohol was hitting him hard, it looked.

"For crying out loud," I said, "can't you see I'm talking to you like a friend?"

He sighed, then ran an arm across his face and swirled his drink.

"How could we be friends?" he said. "I mean, after what's gone down."

"Until we got here, we weren't. But things are different now."

"You're talking Japanese at me here. You know I don't speak Japanese."

His eyes were watering. He'd set his drink on the table and begun to play with his goofy bag.

"It's *before* we got here that things were still cool."

"Before we got here—no—since the day I met you, Jack, since the very instant I met you even, you've been a class-A jerk. I hate to say it like that, but it's true. You're the biggest jerk I ever met."

"I had a serious bad dream last night. *Serious.*"

I let him run his tongue round his mouth.

"I dreamt I dove into a pool," he said, "and stayed down for like an hour, till I couldn't hardly stand it, and when I came up that slime ball was waiting with a stick to crack my skull."

Once again, he looked on the verge of huge despair. I had the sense he was struggling to hold onto his last few strands of self.

"You don't believe in yourself," I told him. "That's why you're a liar. But the thing is, you can't *not* be a liar and face yourself."

173

"Your new boyfriend," Jack said in a last vain attempt to shuffle me off—vain because we both knew it was impossible, now, now he was openly weeping, the tears flowing down his face—"must be feeding you some seriously hairy doses. You're totally flaming, man."

"Look at me, Jack. Really, truly look at me, and tell me *I'm* a liar."

Jack looked at me, all right, but what he said wasn't what I thought I'd hear.

"I saw them," he said. "They were doing it, man, right in front of my face."

"What?"

"I *saw* them," he said. "Jenny and her slime ball. She was socking it to him, man, and totally digging it, like he was God himself. I know I shouldn't have been there, I mean I snuck in there and everything thinking I was going to show her how bogus she was. I was going to show her how pissed off I was, you know, and that she couldn't just screw old Jack Gammler around like he was some farmed out dude from the swamps and shit. I figured maybe if she lost her hair or something she'd know what it was to feel like me, the way she's been torturing me, with all these hardcore trips she's been laying down. I wanted her to know I knew what she was doing. I wanted her to know I wasn't going to keep going round with this rock in my throat. But then they came in, and there was no place to hide, and I couldn't let them catch me booking, so I hid under a couple of towels. And then before I could do anything else, there they were, just like full-on doing it, right there on the floor, right in front of me. It was *horrible*, man, horrible . . ."

The best I could make of Jack's story was that he'd somehow planned to catch Jenny alone in the room before Jomar could return, and shave her bald. But why he'd thought this of all things would bring her back or make Jomar care any less didn't make a lick of sense. Jack was in love with Jenny, who'd spurned him, and this had made of him a buffoon, a pitiful buffoon of love.

"If you believed Jenny wasn't going to be alone," I said, "why were you surprised to find it true?"

Jack tottered for a moment, then collapsed into my arms, moaning.

"But what did I *do*? I know I did something, but I don't know what . . . And, and . . . I don't know, man, where am I supposed to go?"

"It's okay," I said, rocking him. "There's nothing to worry about, Jack. You'll be okay. You *are* okay. Just let it go, now, try to let it go."

He'd become a child, a frightened little boy woken from a dream to find himself alone in a world so bright that without the time to adjust his eyes he could think only of flying again to his nightmare, familiar as it was.

Yet this he couldn't do, either.

The brilliance had shocked him, but the dark of his dream refused him back. He'd been paralyzed, then rejected. He'd no place to go but the sadness of my arms.

I coaxed him to the sofa and wrapped him with a throw.

A Freak Brothers comic lay on the table beside the tray of mixings, along with my new deck of INF cards and some Jean Naté and Breck.

I put the comic and the cards in a drawer and the rest

in the bathroom, then stored the bottles and washed the dishes and lit a candle for Jack.

In my room, in the dark, I got between the sheets. Sleep stole toward me, and forms from the dark—suckling babies, Rosalyn's eyes, a golden foot, the sun.

Happiness was a process, I saw, while the forms kept on.

You are not a thing, Rachel, I thought, *but a* verb.

The rain had passed by the time I rose, and the camp had filled with the perky life that greeted me my first day here.

Naked children frolicked among their naked moms and dads.

A group of women did their calisthenics.

The strangely hairy man I'd seen by the pool walked hand-in-hand with his golden wife, both of them aged but not old, and still, if their faces told a story, very much in love.

A guy sat in trance beneath an ancient tree.

Another, a Spaniard from Perpignan who lost his eye in the Civil War, had thrown himself down to pound his stomach and chest, the end of his daily *regimen*.

Pancakes and bacon filled the air, the smells of toothpaste, lemonade, shower-time soap. I smelled incense, I smelled pipes, I smelled roses and earth and all the trees, the creek down through them, and the moss, the rocks, the mud.

Shouts were in the air, and music, some melancholy harp giving way to a man with a high-pitched voice. *I've been to Hollywood, I've been to Redwood, I crossed the ocean for a heart of gold . . .*

Once again *thingings* had been freshened, made vital and sweet.

The world was *worlding*, and *lovely* was the word, and was all.

Jack was yet asleep. I'd started in on a pot of coffee when I realized I could help him, not from pity but compassion, because being sick—and sick he undeniably was—he needed me, or if not me then someone, a healing presence if nothing else, kindness, yes, endless doses of kindness.

Hadn't Merle done the same for me, given without asking? And had he been here, wouldn't he do for Jack, as well?

But, no, I thought, that wasn't the case at all. Merle wasn't gone, but here, right here beside me, in me and all around me. He'd left for Arcata to talk on the plight of the redwoods and wouldn't be back till night, yet still he was here, still his voice was in my head, still I saw his knowing smile. Merle, I knew, couldn't have left me if he tried. And yes, I thought, I'd draw a bath for Jack.

When all was ready, I jiggled his toe. He didn't know where he was, it seemed, or even, for that matter, me.

"I've drawn a bath for you," I said, and offered him the coffee. "It's ready any time."

The same suspect clarity leapt into his eyes. He mashed a knuckle into one and wrenched.

"Did you put a popper in this joe, or what?"

"You were drunk last night, but not that drunk."

"But you're trying to psyche me out, right? Like as in this is your idea of some killer joke."

"Look outside, Jack. It's gorgeous."

"Dude."

"I made you a nice hot bath, with candles and bubbles and lots and lots of soap. You want to be ready don't you?"

Jack saw the bathroom, the candlelight and suds and shadows on the wall, and it seemed he would faint.

"I don't deserve this," he said.

"I'll be right back," I said.

I went to the pergola and clipped some flowers and placed them in the bottle Merle had used the day he made a bath for me.

Jack was submerged. I'd never seen his face so calm. It was halfway there to water itself.

"There's a lot of fuck-ups in this world, Rachel. I'm one of them, and have been since like forever." He flicked his hands through the suds. "People like me don't deserve this kind of stuff."

"I'm serious, Jack. No more games."

"All I'm trying to do is say I'm sorry."

I scrubbed his back and shoulders and arms and legs. There was only the sound of water on the tub and the laughter of women and men. Jack had abandoned himself, his face had assumed a kind of beauty. Not a David kind of beauty, but its own, the beauty of, what, of release, from some overwhelming debt perhaps.

I was ready to wash his hair when Jenny called my name.

"I don't know about this," Jack said as I left. "I don't know if I can take it."

"I did something terrible," Jenny said.

"Coffee?" I said.

"Thanks a lot, Rachel, but I'm so full of jitters that's the last thing I need right now?"

"Jack is here, you know."

Jenny opened the vitrine and fiddled with the dishes. "Is he all right?"

"He saw you last night. With Jomar."

"I know. I mean that's what I did?"

"Whatever you did is whatever you did."

"But what I did was, I don't know, so mean?" She stepped closer and dropped her voice. "See, I saw him, too. He was in the room when we got there, Jomar and me. I saw him hiding in the corner, and I was so pissed off for that horrible routine or whatever it was he did that I kind of just started doing it with Jomar right in front of him, like on purpose I mean?"

"*You* saw *him.*"

"It was *so* mean, Rachel. We'd come into the room, you know, but just to go to sleep? Then I saw his foot sticking out from a pile of towels but pretended not to and before I knew it I was really, really angry? I thought maybe if he saw us doing it he'd get the picture. I know it was mean, though, and, I don't know, there's like this really big knot in my stomach."

"But *he* doesn't know. That you saw him, that is."

"Don't you think I should tell him? I mean, it's just that I really, *really* hate to lie."

"Believe or not, Jack is fragile."

"But what am *I* supposed to do? I mean, how can I live with myself and all? I feel really terrible, Rachel. Gosh, do you know how bad I'd feel if he ended up hating me? No one's ever hated me, *ever.*"

"He's in love with you," I said. "Or thinks he is."

"Lots of men are in love with me. Maybe you don't understand what a downer that can be."

"You've got nothing to do with who loves you when, and for sure it's not your fault."

"But look what I *do*. Look at *me*. I mean, it's not like I think any more of myself for being so attractive, that's not what I mean, but I really am kind of gorgeous and all, I mean it seems that way from the way everyone treats me, you know, and men are just so, I don't know, sometimes they're just so *silly*?"

I laughed at Jenny's candor, and the truth of her words. It must've been infectious, my laughter, because she began to laugh, as well.

"I guess you'll have to do what you have to do," I said.

Jack had slid into the tub and covered his head with bubbles. All you could see were the caps of his knees.

"Jack?" Jenny said. "Please, Jack," she said when he wouldn't move. "Won't you talk to me?" The water swirled. Jack's hands rose from the bubbles, and then his foamy head. "I know how you feel, Jack. And, well, I guess the only thing I can say is sorry? I really like you, Jack, *really*. But, I don't know, you know, I guess sometimes stuff just kind of happens?"

"*Bull*shit," Jack said.

Jenny blushed. She knew he was right. She'd made things happen as surely as Jack or anyone else. His toes were poking up from the suds by the faucet. Jenny traced them with a finger.

"Do you mind?" she said. "I mean, if I help? I don't

have to like wash you or anything, you know. Or maybe I could just stay here. Maybe I could help Rachel dry you off when you're finished?"

"Are you trying to make *me* feel better, Jenny, or just kill another of your guilt trips? Because you know, man, I don't need your feel-good pity. And hey, let go of my toe already! You might be grooving on some idea I'm a totally humungous worm that can't get himself off the sidewalk after it rains, but I'm here to tell you if that's where you're from, you've got another thing coming. I'm taking care of business, all right? So, seriously, if you're just trying to psyche me out or whatever, you might as well book it. The load I'm trucking here is already totally massive without you coming along to lay *your* stuff on it."

"I do feel guilty," Jenny said. "But that's not why I'm here? I mean, come on, aren't you the one who's always saying it's all about the love?"

"If you love me," Jack said, "I mean if that's the kind of love you're selling, let me tell you, I'm *broke*."

"But I *do* love you, Jack. Maybe not the way you want, but really I do in a terrific way." Jack splashed the water. The light in his face was gone. His hair clung about him, over his dripping beard, and a bead of snot to his nose. "Maybe if you just try and relax?" said Jenny. "And then, when you're done, if you'll let me, I can give you one of my famous massages?" Jack's eyes began to poke about the room. "I'll do an extra super-duper job, too," she said. "Extra fantastic super-duper, Jacky, okay?"

"Swear to God," Jack said, "and tear out your heart if you lie?"

"I swear it, Jack. On my kitten's grave."

"Because I don't know if I could take that. I mean, dude, you totally broke my heart."

"Super, *super*-duper, Jacky. And if you want, I mean if it's not too much or something, I could even dance for you when I'm finished? The bestest most gracefulest dance I ever did?"

Jack flicked a patch of suds onto Jenny's breasts and laughed.

"Where do you come up with that stuff, anyway?"

"Let's wash your hair," I said.

"Yeah," said Jenny, and squeezed the bottle till shampoo filled my hand.

"Whoa," Jack said as I worked it in. "That feels like maybe there's a whole pack of fairy queens on my head, in trippy ballet."

Suddenly my fingers felt hot, and Jack began to twitch.

His scalp was burning, he said. Whatever I was doing, it wasn't fun, he said, and could I knock it off pronto, *please*.

And then he was on fire, he cried, he was screaming like a tortured man.

My fingers, I realized, were burning, too, my fingers and hands, the way Jack had said, as if I'd put them in fire.

And what should I see in my hands when I jerked away, like writhing snakes, but clumps of melting hair!

My God, there were practical mounds of the stuff, melting through my fingers!

I screamed, too, then, frantic as Jack, slapping at his head, crying out nonsense, and Jenny was screaming with us, all of us flailing and screaming.

"What is it?" Jenny said. "What's wrong?"

"My hair is melting!" cried Jack. "Oh! Oh my hair! Turn on the water, hurry!"

On his knees, now, he fumbled at the faucet, manically spinning its knobs.

I shoved his head in the water and went at it, but the hair wouldn't stop. It was sloughing from his head across the board, nothing could stop it, for all the water and scrubbing, it kept on, as if truly his hair were melting.

And then I knew it was so, Jack's hair *was* melting, his hair was really melting!

It was stuck to my hands, clinging to my fingers in sticky clumps, I didn't know what to do.

"Oh my God!" I hollered.

"What!" he said. "What is it?"

"Your hair, Jack," said Jenny, "it's falling out. It's falling out, Jacky, and melting, oh my God what's happened, what should we do, what's happened?"

I tried to turn up the water but the water was tapped, so I scrubbed and flailed till the hair diminished and finally ceased.

Jack sat up, his hair was gone.

There was nothing but gluey clumps.

He looked into our faces, back and forth, and began to wail.

Jenny winced, and I understood. Probably that was all she'd have done, but when Jack's wailing grew, she leapt to her feet and threw a towel on his head and held him close. For a long while she held him there, massaging his poor head, cold comfort that it was. The man could not be soothed.

When at last she removed the towel, to my amazement, to *our* amazement—as if amazement itself could be amazed—there on Jack's scalp we saw it, hidden for years, a birthmark in the shape of a perfect heart.

That was it, I thought, that was why she'd named him so, Jack's mother, that was why she'd called him *my little Jack of Hearts*!

The man had been born with a mark on his head in the shape of a heart that for his whole life he'd never known, a secret across the years to all the world but one.

Jack stumbled to the mirror, now, and began to weep afresh.

For a long motionless instant, he stared at his head with varnished eyes. Then he saw the bottle of Breck, and gaped at it like a thing lost so far back its return might drive him mad.

His mouth fell open, just a parting of the lips really, and what emerged as a chuckle burst into cackling madness. The man was laughing so hard, he was so furiously mad with laughter that soon he was choking. He actually dropped to the floor with his fit, he was actually pounding on the floor with his fists as he cackled and coughed and choked.

"You used *this*," he spurted, and snatched the shampoo up. "*This*, right, it's what you guys put on my hair?"

Neither Jenny nor I said a word. I'd poured shampoo into Jack's hair, then watched his hair melt in my hands. What could we say?

"Do you dudes have any idea what this is?" Jack said. "It says Breck, but it's not, ha ha ha, because it's *Snair*, ha ha ha, a bottle of freaking Snair!" He had got up for a moment, but now he was down again, gawking at the bottle. "Serves me right," he said, "doesn't it? Ha. Ha ha ha. You bet it does, ha ha, it serves me fucking-A right. Ha ha ha ha ha ha ha ha ha ha! You won't believe it," he stuttered, "but this, Jenny—ha ha ha ha ha!—this is the stuff I was going to plant on your ass. It was your shampoo, but I filled it with Snair! To sabotage you with, ha! But check it out. It's me who got it, man. I'm the one who's bald! Ha ha ha! Ha ha ha ha ha!"

I got the frame for Jomar's mirror.

"See this, Jack?"

He looked through the frame, and then at me. A goofy sparkle appeared in his eye, but just the same I held his gaze.

"Your poor mirror!" said Jenny. "What happened?"

"It broke," I said. "I broke it."

"But isn't that, I don't know, supposed to bring really bad luck?"

"It'll bring whatever you say. Won't it, Jack?"

Jack rubbed his head, grinning like a boob. "Ten minutes ago, I'd have told you anything I thought you'd want to hear. Or maybe I'd have said you'd been spiked with dust. But now I don't think there's any such thing as luck."

"Look, Jack," I said. "Stop talking and just *look*."

"There's nothing here but a fancy hunk of wood."

I set the frame on the counter. I took Jack's face and kissed it. What he made of it I couldn't say. I'd simply taken a chance, though immediately I knew he understood. His face was empty of that crazy gleam, now, so wonderfully vacant you could almost have called it a face of peace.

"I'm hungry," I said. "What do you guys say we get cleaned up and head to the Wagon?"

"Hey, gosh, Rachel, that sounds really fantastic?"

"I'll be out in a sec," Jack said. "I've got something to do."

Fifteen minutes later he emerged, hairless as an egg.

By Ned, as Merle would've shouted, the man had even shaved his eyebrows!

And still there, inscrutable as ever, was the birthmark on his head, like an old tattoo, *a little purple heart*.

"I'm ready," he said.

"Oh my God, Jacky, you look so, gosh, I don't know, *interesting*?"

Jack smiled and took our hands.

"Henceforth," he said, "I reserve the right to be human. Let's boogie."

"Yes," I said, "let's," and we stepped through the door.

The "new" Jack's reception was as astounding as my own. The moment we left the cottage, people by the dozen flocked his way. It was as though he'd been swept from fool to sage with the blow of a breath from God. And no one could deny it. He was no more the man he'd been than an infant is a miser.

People brought us soya steaks and mushroom burgers and dosas and ghee, and carob-coated raisins, and carrot juice, and lemon iced tea, and booze.

We gamboled in the pool, played ping-pong and checkers and capture the flag, and danced in the meadow, cloud nine come true: Jomar and Jenny and Merle and Jack, Rosalyn and the baby, Wolfgang and Usch, Willow, Blonda, Fakih.

The annual gala was happening tomorrow, someone said that night, the Saturday nearest solstice, and what was more, another said, the moon would be fuller than our bellies.

Jack stopped me on the path before we parted. "Thank you," he said.

"It's okay," I said. "It's all okay."

"If it weren't for you, I'd be under a bridge."

"And if it not for you, I'd be in my house."

The day began with a cookout round a table thirty feet
long and three inches thick, loaded with anything breakfast
a person could want—sausage from Wisconsin, bacon
from Quebec, waffles and crepes and Quiche Lorraine.
There were biscuits and gravy, French toast and syrup, and
plates full of melons and grapes. And cream tartlets and
corned-beef hash, and soufflés and skillet cakes and bagels
by the bag, we ate it to the crumbs. And the laughter—
wow!—was ceaseless.

And then the games began. The three-legged race
was won by a pair with prosthetic legs. Children bobbed
for apples and got dunked in a machine. I don't know
how, but in the potato-sack race I managed to bounce
my way across the line and was given a Mr. Potato Head.
Hundreds of us formed a snake, each holding the waist
of the person in front while the one at the head tried
to eat the one at the tail. Piñatas full of candy for the
children and coal for the grown ups hung from every
tree. We played Fox Hunts Squirrel, Poison Cookie, and
Chariot War. We had prizes for winners and losers both.
Goodness, what a time!

In the afternoon people massed for the volley-ball tournament, guided round-robin style. Merle and I got Jomar, Jenny, and Jack for a team. A man spiked a ball into Jomar's face. Jack used his penis to serve, and the crowd went wild. Jenny giggled and danced, though not even that could save us. We lost then left with sand in our hair, glad as ever and slapping each other's rumps.

Finally Wolfgang, the gala's improbably perfect master, announced it was time to vote for the King and Queen of Camp Freedom Lake, and one and all we dashed to the pool.

"Hurry, you peoples!" Wolfgang shouted from a podium mounted on the stage. "This is the times for a glory in this sun! This kings are to be choosed. And this queens also, who will she be this year? Hurry, these must be known right away! All must be known right away!"

Three hundred and forty-two humans had gathered round the pool in a whir of speculation.

"Now," Wolfgang said, waving an envelope before him, "it will announce that this erotical mens will run to the stage when this names are detached. Are all this peoples complete?"

"Break the seal!" someone shouted, and everyone cheered.

Wolfgang drew out a slip of paper.

"Frank Bosley!" he shouted, and a roar went up as a muscular man with gold chains round his neck stepped onto the stage.

"Yes," Wolfgang said, "and where is this mans Jomar Links?"

Jomar stood up and raised his arms.

"Dig it, man," he said, "this is awesome!"

Wolfgang was clearly enjoying his role. "Yngwe Jurgenson," he said, "we must have this mans right away! Hurry, Yngwe, hurry to these stage!"

After he'd announced three or four others, Merle among them, Wolfgang said, "And now this last erotical mans, you hurry to these stage, Jack Gammler!"

At this the crowd exploded. So far as I could see, Jack might've learned he'd lost a nickel or won a bag of corn. His face was peaceful as a monk's. By the time he reached the stage, the crowd was on its feet.

"Jack! Jack! Jack!" they chanted.

Wolfgang fanned his arms to calm them, but the people wouldn't stop. Finally he shouted into the microphone.

"Is this the kings that you peoples have decided, Jack Gammler?"

"Long live the King!" roared the crowd. "Long live King Jack!"

"Then this kings is decided!" Wolfgang exclaimed. "Jack Gammler, these peoples has decided that you are to be this kings of Camp Freedom Lake for all of these year of 1973! Kneel on your knees, King Jack, for these crown of erotical flowers!"

A woman approached with a wreath on a pillow, with which Wolfgang crowned our Jack, king, now, for a day.

"You are now these kings!" he announced, and handed him a scepter of wood. "This thrones is there for you to go now!"

Jack rose grinning and seated himself on a high-backed chair wound about with the lilies of his crown.

"King Jack! King Jack! King Jack!" roared the crowd. "Long live the King!"

"And now," Wolfgang said, "all this peoples must have a queen to love for this years also!" He opened another envelope and said, "There are no other names on this slips of paper but one. Do we know now that this peoples have decided these queens already?"

To my complete astonishment, the crowd began to chant my name.

"Rachel! Rachel! Rachel!"

"*Ra*chel Hill," Wolfgang said, "you have been noticed! You are this most erotical womans at the Camp this years, and for these, the peoples have decided for you to be their golden queens. Hurry, *Ra*chel! Run to these place and kneel on your knees for me to give this crowns of erotical flowers!"

It simply couldn't be, I thought, my God it simply couldn't.

And yet I had no choice.

Jomar and Merle had taken me on their shoulders and carried me to the stage. The roar was so deafening I couldn't hear my voice begging them to stop. Then I was set before Wolfgang and the man beside, one of the kingly nominees, with the pillow they'd used for Jack, only my crown was made of roses. I shook my head and tried to speak, but Wolfgang wouldn't have it.

"*Ra*chel Hill," he said, and placed the wreathe on my brow, "you are now this queens of Camp Freedom Lake for all this years of 1973! Long live the Queen! Long live Queen *Ra*chel!"

For a moment I didn't know where I was. I couldn't

see, smell, or hear or taste. A feeling ran through me, of weirdly splendid joy, and I laughed and couldn't stop.

"Queen Rachel! Queen Rachel! Queen Rachel!" roared the crowd. "Long live the Queen!"

Jomar was beside me still, and Merle. Then Jack was there, too, with Wolfgang, and together they fetched me to the diving board.

I mounted the board, and turned to face the crowd.

I waved at the crowd, and the crowd cheered and cheered.

And then, without thought, I leapt into the air.

There I was, poised in glory, nameless faces smiling, the sky above the roaring cheers, endless and blue, water in the distance, shimmering, clear, and blue.

My God, I thought, I was *flying*.

GRATITUDE

Everyone I've already ever thanked, but here and especially:

Jeanine Durning, Michele Filgate, Brandon Hobson, Joshua Mohr, Jordan Rothacker, Nelly Reifler, Christine Sneed, Sarah Gerard, Vi Khi Nao, Alex Mar, Christopher Roman, Penina Roth, Augustus Rose, Mary Miller, Matthew Binder, Sari Botton, Jen Doll, Janet Steen, Charles Bock, Rachel Dini, Matt Pucci, Shana Olson, Jaime Fountaine, Jensen Beach, *Post Road*, Matthew Specktor, Mary South, Jerry Wilson, Lance Olsen, Daulton Dickey, David Leo Rice, David Gutowski, Leza Cantoral, John Domini, David Breithaupt, Michael T. Fournier, Julie Hart, Matt E. Lewis, Michael Shattuck, Rob Hart, Jocelyn Tobias, Will Chancellor, Michael J. Seidlinger, Dennis Cooper, Tobias Carroll (and *Volume One Brooklyn*), Dean Hundley, Luke Silver, Joseph Grantham, Jen Michalski, Joe Winkler, Brentley Frazer, D. Harlan Wilson, Michael Reiter, Kurt Baumeister, Duncan Barlow, Tom Williams, Tyler Malone, Courtney Maum, Amy Shearn, Ben Woodard, Kevin Catalano, J.S. Breukelaar, Eric Larson, Darley Stewart, Seb Doubinsky, Gabino Iglesias, Joanna C. Valente, Matt Bialer, Jeff Jackson, Snorri Sturluson, Christopher O'Brien, Nick Petrulakis, Anderson Berry, Brian Bennett.

Extraordinary props go out to my publisher Stalking Horse Press and the man who runs it, James Reich, who believed in me when no one else would. Eternal gratitude, my friend.

ABOUT D. FOY

D. Foy is the author of the novels *Made to Break* and *Patricide*. His stories, poems, and essays have appeared in *Guernica, Literary Hub, Salon, Hazlitt, Post Road, Electric Literature, BOMB, The Literary Review,* and the *Georgia Review,* among many others, and have been included in the books *Laundromat, A Moment's Notice,* and *Forty Stories: New Writing from Harper Perennial.*

www.dfoyble.com